CALIBAN'S HOUR

Tad Williams is the author of the bestselling
MEMORY, SORROW AND THORN trilogy:
The Dragonbone Chair, *Stone of Farewell* and *To Green
Angel Tower* . A John W Campbell Award finalist, he has
worked as a radio talk-show host, journalist, technical writer,
illustrator and cartoonist. Tad Williams lives in London.

CALIBAN'S HOUR

Tad Williams

Interior illustrations by author

LEGEND

Published in the United Kingdom in 1995 by Legend Books

3 5 7 9 10 8 6 4

First published in the United Kingdom in hardback in 1994 by

Legend Books
20 Vauxhall Bridge Road, London, SW1V 2SA

Random House Australia (Pty) Limited
20 Alfred Street, Milsons Point, Sydney,
New South Wales 2061, Australia

Random House New Zealand Limited
18 Poland Road, Glenfield
Auckland 10, New Zealand

Random House South Africa (Pty) Limited
PO Box 337, Bergvlei, South Africa

Random House UK Limited Reg. No. 954009

A CIP catalogue record for this book is available from the British Library

Papers used by Random House UK Ltd are natural, recyclable products made
from wood grown in sustainable forests. The manufacturing processes
conform to the environmental regulations of the country of origin

Printed and bound in Great Britain by Cox and Wyman

ISBN 0 09 926171 5

This book is dedicated with love to Deborah, who gave me the compass for the journey. I never dreamed what strange meanderings I would experience before it was finished, or to what brave worlds I would travel, both old and new.

> Exultation is the going
> Of an island soul to sea,
> Past the houses – past the headlands –
> Into deep Eternity –
>
> Bred as we, among the mountains,
> Can the sailor understand
> The divine intoxication
> Of the first league out from land?

Emily Dickinson

PART the FIRST
Naples: Evening

His ENTRANCE

SOMETHING SLID DOWN the side of the wide-bellied ship and into the water, quiet as a stolen kiss. As the shadow bobbed to the surface it disturbed a flock of gulls, who rose shrieking to circle high above the harbour; the last rays of sun from behind the mountain turned them, for a little while, into streaks of dull fire against the evening sky. At last they drifted back to the waves, folded their wings, and settled into watchful bird-sleep. They were not disturbed again. Whatever swam there had gone and the harbour was quiet once more.

Light spilled out of the tavern door onto the muddied stones of the Piazza San Ferdinando as a trio of men stumbled out across the threshold into the more uncertain glare of the piazza torches. Behind them a voice rose in song, a first-night-in-port song, full of drunken hopefulness.

'A lot of slags,' one grunted in dockside

Neapolitan. 'We'll do better at Cuvo's, won't we?'

'The fat one was pretty enough,' his companion offered, running his finger carefully around the rim of the wine jar before lifting the finger to his mouth. 'Well cushioned.'

The first spat. 'A bitch. I heard about her from Sandro.' He took a few loose-jointed steps and the man with the wine jar fell in beside him. 'But there's some worth throwing your money at over at Cuvo's, you'll see.' He turned. 'Sebastiano! What in hell's name are you doing?'

'Pissing,' the third man slurred, propping himself one-handed against the tavern wall. The door had fallen shut again, swallowing most of the light and noise. 'A man's got to piss sometimes, doesn't he?'

The one with the jar laughed. '*Drink it down, piss it out,*' he sang, '*that's the way the money goes . . .*'

'We're going to Cuvo's,' the first man called back. 'Come on, then.' With the wine-bearer in tow, he moved off somewhat unsteadily across the piazza.

Sebastiano, still leaning against the wall for support, contemplated with something like satisfaction the puddle now running down the walkway. As he fumbled himself back into his breeches a dark shape appeared from the shadows beside him, silent and sudden. A calloused hand closed on his wrist. He lost his purchase on the wall and stumbled, but the clutching hand held him up until his feet were beneath him.

As Sebastiano yelped and tried to pull away his

free hand strayed behind his back, groping for the rope-cutter in his belt, but something lashed out from the shadows and imprisoned the other arm. He was held firmly by a large man-shaped shadow whose cloak drizzled water onto the paving stones.

'What do you w-w-want? I've no money. My mate – my mate there –' Sebastiano tried to gesture across the Piazza, but could only twitch a shoulder, '– he's got my purse.'

The shadow figure said something guttural and urgent that the drunken sailor could not understand. He again tried to tear himself free, but his wrists were held as though manacled. The pressure increased. Sebastiano squealed in pain.

'What do you want? Ah! *Santa Maria*!' He caught a glimpse of the eyes hidden in the shadowed hood and his legs slowly folded beneath him until he knelt before the dripping shape.

Again the thing questioned him; this time he could almost understand the rough speech, but his heart was beating so fast he was sure it would burst and he could not think properly. At last he heard what seemed to be a name, then heard that name said again. The fumes of drink utterly dispersed by terror, the safety of the tavern and his friends both only a few short steps away but completely, hopelessly out of reach, Sebastiano shuddered, then forced himself to repeat aloud the name he thought he had heard.

For a moment, as the grip on his arms tightened so

cruelly that he thought his bones would snap, he was certain he had said the wrong thing; childhood prayers, entreatments saved for storms at sea, whirled in his thoughts. Then the pressure slackened. He looked up to see the eyes in the shadowed face gleam with reflected torchlight, burning steadily as marsh-fire. The thing stared at him, head cocked, listening.

'There.' Sebastiano wagged his head towards a blocky shadow on the skyline, a dark mass crowned with spiky towers. 'Everybody knows,' he gibbered. 'Everybody! There. In the castle.'

The shadow released one of the sailor's hands and lifted a gnarled, pointing finger towards the Castel Nuovo.

'Yes!' Sebastiano wheezed, feeling the thing's fingerprints still in his flesh. He nodded his head weakly. 'There. There.'

A moment later he was alone. Trembling so badly he could not stand unaided, he leaned against the cold stone wall and wept. The torches still fluttered around the piazza. The shadows were empty.

As the tavern door swung inward, his shipmates jeered.

'Thought you went off to Cuvo's place with old Too-Good-For-Us,' one shouted. 'Or did you lose your way?'

Sebastiano staggered towards the fire and took his place on a bench there. Shivering, he stared at the livid finger-marks on his sunbaked arms. His fearful, distracted face eventually brought a sort of quiet down on the crowded room.

He looked up from his bruises and into the depth of the flames, as though he were alone in the tavern. The tears on his cheek were drying rapidly in the heat of the fire.

'I have met the Devil tonight,' he rasped. 'Heaven save me. His eyes are yellow . . . and he stinks of fish.'

The CASTLE

NIGHT NESTLED IN the crevices between the stones of the castle's great archway gate.

A pair of sentries talked in low tones, pikes sagging, cloaks wrapped tight against the chill. When they finally retreated into the gateway to shelter from the ever-colder wind, a large shadow detached itself from the darkness like a piece of black velvet torn from heavy drapery, then clambered swiftly up the angled corner where the tower met the gate. Within a half-dozen heartbeats it was far above the shivering guardsmen, mounting the face of the arch like a spider.

Dark fingers clutched the silent heads of the statues; muscles bunched and extended as the figure drew itself upward, finding handholds and toeholds in the details of the carved reliefs, pawing the dignified stone faces of saints and warriors. At last the climber reached the top of the arch and stood there, cloak billowing and faintly silvered by moonlight.

As it paused, unmoving, to look down on the Castel Nuovo's inner keep, there was a trace of the simian in its posture, in the hunched shoulders and the curve of the great, powerful arms. There was something equally animal in the way it leaned forward, rigid and intent as a hunting beast scenting its prey.

The keep's upper windows glimmered like eyes, but they were blind eyes. No alarm was given as the shadow-shape dipped into a crouch, then began to make its way down into the inner courtyard.

A DOMESTIC Scene

'GIULIETTA, I WILL hear no more of it. This is your father's wish; there is nothing I can do.'

She was attired for sleep in a nightdress of Cathayan silk, but there was nothing of rest in her attitude. Her fine-boned face was drawn into tight planes and creases of worry, and she clutched the blankets with her thin fingers.

Pacing back and forth beside her bed was a girl just on the edge of womanhood, whose swirl of dark hair, unbound for the night, swayed like the tail of an uneasy horse.

'I am the second-to-the-last child, Mother.' The girl's voice would have been sweet but for the angry, self-pitying tone of her words. 'You have married off two daughters already, and Naples has an heir. Why should my life be caught up as well?'

'He is an able young man, and not unhandsome. Oh, merciful Lord, how my head hurts! Please,

Giulietta, your father has thought very carefully . . .'

'My father has thought very carefully about what will suit him, not me! What do I care for young Ursino or any of his family?'

The woman on the bed drew in breath sharply. 'Have a care how you speak of your father!' Her voice trembled. 'The world has not changed so much that . . . that daughters may insult their sires without retribution.' She paused and looked down at her slender hands clutching the coverlet. 'From Heaven, I mean. For surely it is a sin to flout the father who loves you and cares for you.'

'Does he? I can scarcely recall what he looks like, he is here so seldom.' She hesitated, but only for an instant. 'I am surprised you even remember that you are married.'

'*Giulietta*! If I had said such things about my . . . even *thought* such things . . . !'

The girl stopped pacing. She clenched her fists and opened her mouth wide as though for another angry denunciation. Instead she shuddered, then flung herself down beside the bed. She pressed her forehead against the quilt, against her mother's hip, and wept. 'I cannot breathe! I have dreams that I am buried alive – terrible nightmares! I do not want to marry Renato Ursino! Oh, Mama, I am so miserable!'

The woman reached out a hand to stroke her daughter's dark hair. 'But what can possibly make you so unhappy, my rabbit? I beg you, tell me. He is said to be sweet-tempered, and his family's house is very close — you will not be far from all you love.'

'But that's just it! I have seen nothing! Done nothing! And now I will go to live in the house of the Ursino family, and I will have babies . . . and then I will grow old, and I will die.'

Her mother laughed in pained surprise. 'But darling one! There is far more that will happen to you than that. And having babies is nothing to sniff at. My life would mean little without you, my dear, and all the rest of my brood.'

'You had a life before. I have had nothing, seen nothing. I am *smothering*!' Giulietta's anguished words were muffled against her mother's lap.

'What you know of my childhood is exaggerated, misleading. I was often frightened . . .'

The girl lifted her tearstained face, eyes suddenly bright. 'I would *love* to be frightened! Grandfather took you across the ocean. You saw a whole new world! I will die here, among the same faces I have seen my entire life, in dreary, gossipy Naples!'

Before her mother could reply they were startled by a knock on the bedchamber door. One of the ladies-in-waiting poked her head in, then quickly stepped back again to admit an old woman carrying a very small boy.

'I beg your pardon, Highness.' The old woman paused to dart a stern, meaningful look at the daughter. 'I know you like to be left alone at bedtime, but he can't sleep for having nightmares. Asked for you over and over.'

'Of course, Francesca.' The mother held out her arms and the boy was delivered, eyes half-closed, fair hair mussed and damp with night-sweat. 'What is it, little Cesare?' she asked, stroking his red face. 'Why are all my chickens so uneasy tonight?'

'Man, man.' Cesare waved his fat little hand.

'He thinks he saw a man at the window,' the nurse said fondly. 'Kept pointing and crying.'

'Oh, he has had a bad dream, the poor little thing.' His mother kissed the dried tears on the boy's cheeks. 'Cesare, there is no man outside the window. It's too high up in the air!' She sang to him for a while, then at last turned to old Francesca. 'Look, I think he's falling asleep again.'

Giulietta had stealthily wiped her face dry, and now she stood. Her angry gaze went from the nurse to her mother. 'He would sleep better if he didn't eat so many sweets.'

'Yes.' Her mother nodded, smiling as though Giulietta's tone had been less harsh. 'He is spoiled indeed, the poor little thing.'

'There,' said the nurse. 'You're right, Highness, he's dropped off again already. A mother's touch.' She spoke with the satisfaction of an alchemist whose experiment confirms a great universal truth. 'A mother's touch.'

The lady of the house was about to surrender the sleeping child to his nurse, but abruptly turned instead to her daughter. 'Why don't you take him back and put him to sleep, dear? He is so very fond of you. Besides, it is time for you to be abed yourself, my rabbit.'

Giulietta glared, but took the child. 'You mean it is *your* bed-time,' she grumbled. 'It is scarcely an hour past sundown.'

Her mother did not argue. 'I have been tired since this last one came. Go on, take him, Giulietta. Help Francesca put him to bed. It would be a kind thing to do.'

The girl made a face, but took the open-mouthed, faintly snoring child with suitable care and followed after the nurse. She turned in the doorway.

'I will not sleep just because you tell me to,' Giulietta said in a loud whisper. 'And I will *not* marry Renato Ursino!'

Her mother waved her out, gently but firmly. 'We will talk about that some other time. Please tell Amelia I am going to sleep now.'

When the door was closed and the chamber empty, Giulietta's mother sank back against the pillows with a deep sigh, then turned and blew out the candle on the bedside table. The dying fire cast a few long shadows. The bone-white moon hung framed in the window.

The VILLAIN

THE ECHOES OF the church bells tolling the eleventh hour were fading when the bedchamber door opened on silent hinges. A dark shape moved through, then pushed the heavy door back into place. The smouldering embers in the fireplace painted red along the edges of everything.

The shadow approached the bed and for a long time stood motionless, surveying the sleeping woman. At last, as though the force of such scrutiny had penetrated her dreams, the woman's eyes fluttered open and wandered for a moment unfixed before widening with alarm.

'What . . . ?' she gasped. 'Who . . . ?'

A dark hand sprang from beneath the figure's cloak and covered her mouth. She struggled, but even with both her own hands she could not push away the clamping fingers.

The shape leaned closer. Her wide eyes became even rounder and her thrashing movements increased. 'I will let you go.' The deep voice spoke Milanese, with strange undertones. Astonishingly, the prowler did not whisper, as though he – for no female throat could birth such a chesty rumble – did not fear discovery. 'I will let you go,' he continued, 'and you may shout until you echo the hurricane. But even if you manage to wake someone to help you – although I am certain there is no one nearby so capable – then you will merely bring yourself a swifter ending.'

His lifted hand vanished into the cloak like a black rabbit going to ground. She pulled herself back against her pillows, as far from the intruder as she could shrink. 'You are from . . . Milan?' She was hardly able to speak for breathlessness.

He laughed, but there was pain in it. 'So you recognise your native speech, but you do not remember me, Miranda? I suppose I am not surprised.' He threw back the hood of his cloak to reveal a shaggy-haired head set low and tilted forward on short neck and broad, muscle-knotted shoulders. His skin was tanned and leathery. Beneath his heavy, bony brows his eyes glinted as shockingly yellow as an owl's.

Miranda raised her trembling hands to her face. '*Caliban* . . . .?'

He laughed again, harshly, and slapped his hands together with a crack loud as a musket shot, then bared his long, crooked teeth and did a strange dance, capering like a beggarman's monkey. 'Ha!

So you do remember! I have survived – I *exist*! – at least as a memory.' He stopped and leaned close, curling his lips. 'At least as a nightmare.'

Miranda shook her head, dazed. 'But what . . . why are you . . . after all these years . . . ?'

'Why am I here?' He smirked. 'Why, to kill you, of course.' He spread his great arms as if to applaud her terror. 'Go to, then. Scream until the rafters shake. It will only hasten your end. But if you love life so that you fear to leave it, then I advise you to stay quiet and thus make full use of what you have left.'

Miranda let out her pent breath; for a moment she had to struggle to take another. 'You mean to slay me?'

He crouched. 'Nothing so simple or so sudden, little queen. I could have murdered you in your sleep if I chose, snuffed you as easily as you extinguished this taper.' He plucked the candle from her bedside table and backed towards the fire, then held the wick in the embers until it caught. As he returned he held it close, so that it threw the thick bones of his brow into stark relief. 'One pinch, then blackness,' he said, setting it down once more. 'But that would be too swift; it would not serve me. I have gone to great effort to come here, Miranda. "Heroic" might not be too bold a word: I have ridden in the damp, fish-perfumed, rat-swarming holds of ships; I have swum miles through cold, shark-sliced water; I have risked the swords of city men. Yes, "heroic" might indeed be the word . . . if there could ever be a hero as ugly and spiteful as I am. We must be careful with our words, after all — they are very important. In fact, they have brought me here.'

'Words?' Miranda sat up straighter. 'I do not understand.'

'Do you not? I . . . have . . . *words* . . . for you.' He took a step forward and clutched her wrist. 'Your father is dead.'

She shook her head at the pain of his grip. 'Five years. This is no news.'

'It was to me.' His lips curled in a snarl. 'Two decades I roamed that empty island in bleak, abject misery. Twenty black years, and all I could think was that someday I would find your father again and tender him the payment I owed him. At last I escaped — it was not easy, Miranda! — and made my way to Milan. But he is dead! Prospero is dead! Who could have imagined my iron-boned tormentor might grow old and die like an ordinary man? Not all the force of my bitter hatred can bring him back. He has cheated me.' His hand tightened again. 'But you have not.'

'Cheated you? Of revenge?'

'Yes. Oh, yes. I have been robbed of a chance to make him hear the words he gave me put to their necessary use. Cheated of an hour in which I could make him hear my grievances, every last one. It is the final betrayal. May his soul twitch in the fires of Hell, if such a place does exist. Of all the things he taught me, that is one I hope does not prove a lie, as so much else did. May his soul *burn*.'

Miranda traced the sign of the cross. Caliban laughed.

'You should look to your own soul, pretty Miranda.'

'So you will kill me.'

'You do not seem suitably frightened. Is your current life so miserable?' He narrowed his eyes, then smiled. 'Ah, I see you stealing glances towards the door. Do you anticipate rescue from the guardsman? Sadly, old Somnambulo – for that must be his name: I could have walked past him whistling had I chose – is now sleeping even more deeply than his usual wont. I gave him a goose-egg on the back of his head, but I imagine he will recover his wits by morning. And I know when the guard will change, and who will take his place. I have been watching for three days, Miranda. I know the rhythms of your house almost as well as I know the tides that play along the beaches of my island . . . our island.'

'Then it was you that Cesare saw!'

His smile grew crooked. 'Your pampered child. I wonder what sort of man he would make if he had been given a life like mine, instead of luxury, cosseting, and a fine lady like yourself for a mother.'

'You will not hurt him!' Now she struggled, and desperately, but he was far too strong. When exhaustion had at last calmed her, Caliban released her wrist. Faint purple marks spotted the skin.

'It is only you, Miranda, whom I sought.' He spoke as though mildly offended. 'Since your father has escaped my justice, it is you who must hear my words.'

'Words. You keep saying . . .'

'Because that was the gift your father gave to me. And the curse that ruined me as well, changed my life to wretched misery. There are hours yet before the guard comes — nay, eons. An eternity, in fact. This is my time, Miranda. Now you will have your words back: before I kill you, you will hear my tale . . . and you will know what you have done.'

'But . . .'

'*Silence!*' His roar was so loud that for a moment, in the echoing stillness that followed it, both waited expectantly. Then Caliban chuckled. 'You see? There is no one to interrupt us. Your guard is insensible, the household asleep. Your husband — unremarkably, from what I have heard — is in another city. Parading his rule before some of his most admiring subjects, no doubt.' He showed broad teeth. 'In truth, everyone seems to have someone else tonight, Miranda. Your maid Amelia is with her swain, one of the soldiers. I do not doubt you have turned a blind eye to that — young love is a charming thing, is it not? And we are also a pair, we two. So you *will* hear me, even if I must lay rough hands on you to ensure your attention.'

He stood, a vast and looming shadow but for the gleam of his eyes.

'You will listen now, Miranda. You will hear the sound of my secret heart before I destroy you. And before you travel into darkness, you will know just what you have done. *You will listen . . .*'

PART the SECOND
The Villain's Tale

A MOUTH full of WORDS

WHAT SHOULD I say, Miranda – now that the time has come, what should I tell you? How? What? Where do I begin? I have been clamp-jawed with silence so long; now it must all rush out. The words inside me can be pent no longer, and it is you who must brave the torrent. I cannot promise you will not be drowned by its raging force.

There – do you see? That is one of the chief crimes with which I charge you and your father . . . especially your father. You two brought me a gift, or so I thought, a shining object like a bright fruit dangled in front of a starveling: you taught me that all things have names. Your gift to me was words – a language. But it was a poison fruit, that naming-of-things, for with language I learned lies.

Conceits, tricks, prestidigitations – and see! I perform them too! There is no rushing torrent of water, only a story that I will tell. A river is a river, wet, noisy, a home for fish and whirring, winged flies

25

and skimming beetles. It is not made of words — in fact, a great part of its beauty is that it has no words at all. But your father and his spreading canker of a language — there, witness! I am a prisoner of his lying comparisons still! — first named, then took the meaning from everything.

Before you came, I lived in a world of certain, solid truths, Miranda. 'Bestial' is what your kind calls that world, that way, but I am not so sure. I have now seen your cities, the streets and dockside teeming with pale people hurrying like termites in a split log. With so many crushed together, and each one telling a thousand tiny lies in an hour, lying with every breath, every glance, can you tell me that my isolation and simplicity were worse?

On my island I existed in a world of unquestionable *things*. The great rock above the beach had no name, but I knew it, and knew what it was: something upon which I could climb to see far out across the ocean's face. A family of lizards nested there, small, brown, striped with yellow, and though they fled before my approach, skittering into crevices to lie in silent panic until I passed them by, I did not think of them as being more alive than the great stone, or of some higher order of being — no more than I thought so of myself. They moved, I moved; the rock did not. And yet, sometimes an entire afternoon passed when both lizards and I were as still as the great shelf of stone — while, for all I knew, perhaps there were times when the stone

itself walked, or crawled, or even flew, and I simply had not seen such a moment.

In my mind, that great rock was a thing, just as the lizards were things, each one, and I did not try to compare it with anything else. It simply was. *I* simply was. The objects I found on my island were food if I could eat them, shade if I could sleep beneath them. The weather itself was not a separate phenomenon that could be discussed, like war in a distant country. Some days the world was wet and windy. Other days the entire universe sweltered in unchanging heat.

In fact, it was on just such a day, a day when the whole of creation seemed a stone baking in the coals of a fire, that I climbed the great rock and saw my doom.

Could I have hidden from what proved to be my fate? The island was not large, but there were enough high places, enough hidden, frond-shaded folds, that perhaps I could have kept my distance, at least for the first year. If I had, I would have thought differently, seen differently. I would have grown a year older and also I would have had the custom of separateness – watching, I would have felt myself a distinct thing; learning, I would have understood differently.

But, like the lizards, I was fearful but ultimately stupid. Just as they always ran, but never any farther than the same shallow crevices, so I watched my doom walk towards me across the white beach and did no more to save myself than to crouch slightly lower behind a jagged cornice of stone. Up until that moment, with my mother dead, I had been the lord of my land, but now my fall from power was before me. How well your exiled father must have understood that sort of agonising reversal – the rebel hand that strikes by surprise, the fatal mistake perceived too late! But understanding did not make him treat me any better in later days.

Two figures, one large, one small. I cannot say, Miranda, that I saw you and instantly fell in love with you, poignant as that might be. I think I was yet too young. I believe, but I am not sure, that I had been alive perhaps a decade when you landed. Of course, the chance to know the details of my early life, including my birth-year, were lost even before I was born, vanished along with my mother's tongue. Lost with my mother tongue.

It's true that you fascinated me, with your tired little body, your damp hair, your bright dress all in rags, but it was your great, gaunt father whose aspect set all my hairs standing like the itch of distant lightning.

At first he was just a pillar of black on the sun-whitened beach, standing before a grounded boat. I had a moment of dreamy confusion, for I thought the two of you had stepped from *our* boat, even though I knew that the craft which had brought my mother into exile had rested on another part of the beach, and had long since been plundered of everything but a few rotted timbers.

Prospero. Could ever your God have appeared to His followers with any greater effect? I had never seen a grown man before of any sort – had, at that moment, never seen another human creature except my mother and my own reflection in the island's pools. And there stood your father, far taller than I was, wrapped in a black robe that must have felt like the inner walls of a kiln on that blazing hot day. But as if to confirm his magical, unnatural state, his beard seemed to me a stream of grey and black hoarfrost hanging from his jaws, ice such as I sometimes found on the leaves and rocks of the island's high places during the coldest months. His eyes, too, were frosty as he surveyed the beach, then slowly looked up to the rock where I crouched so poorly hidden: chips of a blue darker and yet brighter than the sky, they glinted from beneath heavy brows. Altogether, he seemed a thing of iron, like the nails we had salvaged from our boat, cold and unyielding, sharp and black. A creature of iron and ice.

But there – I have run ahead of myself, and I see I have confused you. Unstoppered, I have gushed, when all should instead be poured out into careful measures. For each part of this story has a different taste, and if you would know what I know, if you would understand what I feel, even a little, you must be given each draught in its proper turn. But, oh, Miranda, how hard it is to wait. The bung has been in the cask for twenty years; the wine inside has corrupted into swirling fumes and vinegar. But wait I shall, and try to tell the story proper. But wait.

You do not remember Sycorax, my mother. Of course you do not – she died choking on a fishbone, bulge-eyed and empurpled, two years before you came to my island. I remember her unnaturally well. For the largest part of my young life she was the only voice I knew, though she spoke to me only in grunts, the only other creature in any way like myself. She was the bold sun that overhung my landscape as well as the ominous moon whose light made me shiver and hide beneath my blanket of leafy branches. Until your father spun into the heaven of my understanding like a dark lodestone star, she was my only constellation.

I worshipped her, I feared her, I hated her. I loved her until it burned me inside. And she in turn was the only living creature who has ever loved me. She was mad, that woman, swollen like a ram-fed goose on her own contradictions. She could spend an afternoon carefully skinning and pithing a fennel stalk to reveal to me how God's green children drink, then box my ears until I wept for the crime of curiosity, for annoying her with my needs, for tugging at her elbow to show her some wonder I had discovered. She stared at the sky sometimes and laughed without sound. She drew fantastically intricate pictures in the sand, then rubbed them out with her feet the moment they were finished.

She was a witch, my squint-eyed, sharp-nosed mother. I did not know the word – I did not know *any* words until your father planted them in me like hard little seeds – but I knew from the dreams she shared with me that she was not like others. To a child, his mother must always be a creature of power, a possessor of arcane knowledge, of healing arts and painful curses, but it was not only her son who saw her thusly. They banished her, you know. They silenced her and drove her away.

She was driven out of Algiers. Not surprising: she *was* a witch, after all. She was proud of it – of the black lessons she had learned, the scraping and scuffling after obscure knowledge, the nervous, averted eyes of her neighbours that reflected her own dark eminence back to her. But power, eminence, these are dangerous possessions. Your own father found that out, Miranda, did he not? They arouse envy. They inspire whispers. Those who fear and placate you wait only to see you misstep, then they are upon you like wolves on a once-proud stag grown old and infirm.

My mother, for all her cleverness and untutored politics, made such a mistake. The snare pulled tight. She was denounced, rolled through the public square in a tumbrel, then sentence was passed by the mayor. The whisperers had overthrown her, but they still feared – that much at least her dark arts bought her. They were terrified of her dying curse. And well they should have been, the wives who stood beside the husbands my mother had caught for them with night-gathered herbs, the farmers grown fat on the flesh of swine she had cured of the hissing sickness. Even the mayor himself had only been elevated to his post after he had visited my mother's house under cover of darkness one night: his predecessor pitched over dead the following day. Hypocrites! If I am glad of anything, it is that I did not spend my childhood among such creatures.

So frightened were they of her magical words, her curses, that they scorched out her tongue with a fire-heated iron – but even that was not enough. Afraid that the killing of even a silenced witch would bring a plague of bad luck down on them, they put her in a boat, my pregnant mother, and towed her out to the open sea where she was set adrift.

Pregnant, yes. Heavy with child, and no man to claim the fathering. The wild, conflicting rumours about the sire's identity helped spread my mother's ill fame far beyond the place where she had lived.

If God would see you preserved, that treacherous imp of a mayor said from the other boat as she drifted away, *then He will bring you safe again to some far shore*.

How do I know these things, if my mother had no

tongue to say them? Because your father told me. He had known of my mother's banishment, although to him it had been no more than a bit of gossip, some idle chat from a merchant fisherman wintering in Milan. And here again your father put a curse upon me, for now all my memories of my mother, the only creature who truly cared for me, are strained through the sieve of Prospero and his cursed language – just as are the words I speak to you now, pouring out my heart! He took my past and he took my future. He drove me into a dark burrow and then stopped it at both ends. May his soul twist and burn forever!

But he did not know all. There are things I had before I had his words. Some of my mother's story still remains to me, and only now do I corrupt it with the rot of speech. She was put to sea, heavy with me – with Caliban unborn. Our boat drifted and drifted. One kindly woman, a neighbour, had secreted a few small loaves of bread and a jar of water in the boat, and this kept my mother – and me, I suppose – alive as the boat wandered errantly across the ocean. At first my mother employed the singed stub of her tongue to curse – great wordless curses that made the very clouds overhead curl and blacken along their edges. Soon, though, she had too little strength for cursing. By the time a week had passed, she could do nothing but lie in the boat's bottom, her shawl draped over her head to shade her from the sun, and wait for death.

But she did not die, Miranda, and because of that I came to be. So blame your God, as one always must, for putting a match to the train of events that will now take you from the arms of your family, just as I blame that God – or Whatever might hold His usurped throne – for sending you and your cursed father into my life, to make it a confusion and a misery.

The island . . . *my* island . . . came into view as a muddy blot on the horizon.

My mother washed up at last and crawled out of the boat and a little way onto the beach, finding there as if set by some provident spirit the shade of some trees and a rill of clean rainfall that ran down from the heights. By those two things, shade and water, she was saved. By those two things was I preserved inside her belly, although I was nothing but a sprat, a minnow, a pollywog.

So, you are wondering, if your father did not know *these* tales, how do I know them now? Much he taught me – some few true things, many lies – but he was not the first to catechise me! I had learning of many sorts at my mother's knee, and though there were no words, I see still the pictures she put in my head, her own thoughts. She did not speak to me at all, and seldom even grunted – what I remember most of her face was a mouth like a pocket that was almost never opened – but somehow there are pictures. I will tell you of that later.

Until I came, she succoured herself in that new

world with the fruit and stupidly overconfident fish and crablets – the same with which we continued to feed ourselves throughout my childhood. For the island was well provided in everything we needed: all necessities were given swiftly and for little cost. As soon as I could walk by myself, I could forage for the prickly fruit with the green rind, or the sweet plantain, or those red sacks of juice that your father called 'wasp-apples', finding and plucking them as easily as bending to pick up a pebble. I feasted, then threw aside stones and seeds; by the time a few moons had turned, new fruit-bushes and trees would be growing there. I ate when I was hungry, slept when I was tired, and except for my mother's whims, lived as free and unthinking as any beast.

I had no name, just as she had not until your father told me – 'Sycorax', he said she was called, and it has ever felt foreign to me. I was not even 'Boy', or 'You', for my mother had no speech. I was a look in her eye that meant 'Come here', a beckoning hand, or at most a grunt, a sound like a sow snuffling in soft earth. That exhalation was my only name until you and your father arrived. It was enough.

I *was*, and I knew it. Who else could it be who saw the lizards on the rock when my mother was not there? Who else ate the fruit my mother did not eat, or climbed the trees that my leathery but brittle mother could not climb? Who else did Sycorax beckon to? I existed, and I needed no name to prove it – unlike those maggoty multitudes creeping and sleeping in Naples below us like identical bees in the slots of a great hive. I was small, but I was the only thing like me. If my mother was my first god, I was her only worshipper, and thus all-important – for what use is a god without devotees?

I have now seen the huge churches of Naples. Although I heard of them from your father, Miranda, and saw pictures in his books, I could not quite believe any building so tall could exist. Now I believe . . . but I still do not understand. If your God is everywhere, if He is always watching, why should your people make houses to go to worship Him? Faced with an all-seeing, everywhere-being God, I would think what is needed is a place to hide.

I had to find such a place on my island. For if my mother was *my* god, she was often a jealous deity. Just as no tie of blood would make her pay notice to me when she did not wish to, so also no complaint or resistance would fend off her attentions when I did not want them. Whether I was eating, sleeping, or moving my bowels, when my mother called for me I was to come, and quickly.

As I grew out of infancy, it seemed that there were countless things I could not do, ways I could not be, faces I could not make. My mother beat me when I annoyed her, although what it was that caused her anger was seldom obvious. Other times she would clutch me and hold me, keening and mumbling in her wordless way, as if I were the only thing that kept her heart from bursting in her breast.

Did I say that I loved her? For I did, helplessly, and no beating ever changed that. Yet still there were times when I could not bear to be with her, as if my very love for her was a hole yawning beneath my feet, threatening to swallow me up.

As I grew older, my need for independence became a strong hunger. If I left in the morning and was gone all day, I would earn a thrashing – but only one. To remain instead by her side was to risk a score of unexpected blows, and just as many equally unexpected – and almost equally disturbing – displays of miserating affection. But she knew the island almost as well as I did. It was not enough to be merely out of reach – if so, any one of dozens of trees or rocks would have sufficed as a shelter. I had to be out of her sight and the sound of her grunting voice as well. It was a strange magic my mother had – perhaps all mothers have it, I do not know – but to be near her was to feel the need to obey her.

There was one particular place that tugged at my attention – a valley. Not strenuously distant from the hut in which my mother and I lived, set in the embrace of the nearest rocky foothills, it was nevertheless one of the few places we had not explored, since the only path down into it was choked by brambles, each branch of which carried thorns as long as the first two knuckles of my finger. Effectively barred to us, it was much in my imagination, and I would often loiter at the top of the path beside the thorn hedge, although there were higher places on the island, spots where the view was better and that were harder for my mother to reach.

One day I was crawling along the top of this path on my hands and knees, following the progress of an insect which looked for all the world like an ambulatory stick. In truth, in my open-hearted acceptance of wonders, I assumed it *was* a stick, just some heretofore unencountered variety that happened to walk. In any case, this particular stick at last turned and blithely strolled into the shelter of the brambles. I stared after it sadly, knowing it was beyond my reach, wishing that *I* could be so small and disappear so easily. But as I looked at the place it had gone, I saw that although the thorny branches entwined too thickly to allow passage for anything much larger than the now-escaped insect, they did not quite touch the ground. Each bramble-bush sprouted from a central trunk, and there were only a half-dozen such trunks across the width of the path, although the tangling made it appear one continuous hedge. I lowered myself onto my belly and saw that there was indeed a space beneath the thorns a little less tall than the width of my palm. I sat up again, disappointed. I was still far too big: even lying flat on my back, I would be scraped bloody and raw before I pushed myself a yard in.

Then a sudden thought sent me scrambling back down the hillside. I searched the ground and soon discovered what I needed: a pair of fallen branches from one of the larger trees, each branch nearly as tall as I was, both relatively straight, especially after I had broken off the smaller cross-limbs. I went back to the thornhedge, pushed the branches under its skirt and lifted. A slightly wider gap opened. Holding the makeshift staves carefully, I rolled onto my back, then slid headfirst into the space. The brambles hung like storm-clouds just above my face, shuddering as the sticks in my hands trembled beneath the weight of the intertwined branches. I gently slid the sticks forward, shutting my eyes in panic for a moment when it seemed as though the suspended bramble might break free and smash down on me, then inched myself further along. Again the sticks held the thorns just high enough, although one or two now grazed my chest, digging as my mother's sharp fingernails did when I overslept.

It was a long and dreadful process. The two sticks grew slippery in my sweaty hands: dust, long undisturbed, sifted down from the bushes into my mouth and nose and eyes, and my muscles grew weak. When I had pushed in the entire length of my body, it occurred to me that I was now trapped: it was virtually impossible to turn around, and should the distance ahead prove to be too far – what if the thorns extended all the way down the valley? – my strength would quickly give out, the brambles would sag down, and I would lie hidden and bleeding until I died.

Crying only made it harder to keep moving, so I did my best to restrain my tears. Even were I to scream for my mother, what could she do? She was tough as a dried fish, and stronger than I was, but it would take days for her to hack such a weight of thorn branches away with her stone knife.

Creeping forward with slow, agonising movements of my shoulders, elbows, and heels, I at last began to feel a stronger light falling on my face. The branches were thinning! Renewed hope brought renewed strength; I pushed on until my face finally appeared from beneath the hedge. The sun dried the sweat and dust into a thin mask of mud on my face as I worked the rest of my body out from beneath the brambles. When my feet came free, scratched and bloody, I rolled onto my side and lay panting in the dirt like the wounded, terrified animal I was.

But youth is resilient, Miranda. You obviously believe that, for did you not send your own girl-child off tonight, certain that those things which gall her so today will be forgotten tomorrow? And the young *are* resilient . . . when they have not been pushed beyond their capability. Thus, it was not long until young Caliban – or young No-Name, as I still was then – was on his feet again, admiring the new lands which his bravery had conquered.

Do you remember that valley, Miranda? I took you there once. Surely you remember that place, that day. Surely.

Beyond the brambles lay a miniature Paradise, an

afterlife to which either Christian or pagan would be glad to awaken. A small stream flowed down the slope beside me, its source hidden in the widening of the thorn hedge. Long grass, a wind-combed crest that reached my knees, lined the stream's path, and spread into a tiny meadow at the bottom of the narrow valley. Around the meadow, like protective spirits, stood a ring of delicate, round-leaved trees. At their centre stood the only object taller than the valley's walls, a huge, ancient pine. I had seen its bristling apex from other high places on the island, but to the extent I had thought of it, I had assumed it grew from some place along the valley's mounting walls. Now I could see that its trunk stretched a good dozen times my height, that its powerful roots had pushed the rocks aside in their growth as casually as an uneasy sleeper kicks away his cloak.

Although everything in the valley was new to me – the tuneful noise of the water, so much gentler and more friendly than the sea's constant grumbling, the hum of sparkling dragonflies darting past my ears – it was the old pine that drew my attention. It seemed to have been waiting for me. In my wordless way, I sensed something of its age, something of its mystery. But not all of its mystery. No, not all.

I made my way down the streambank, the grass-stems scraping at my shins, mud sucking at my toes. Despite the small noises all around, a sense of stillness and power hung over the valley. A thrill ran up the back of my neck. The fact that I had found this place made me feel taller, wider — *more*, somehow: this expansion of my world had caused me to grow as well. It was the first thing in the world that was mine and no one else's. I felt I had come into an inheritance of sorts. It was my first day of manhood.

The stream dwindled into a series of smaller rivulets and at last disappeared in a delta of matted grass. I squelched across it towards the base of the pine tree and found a place where the sun arrowed down and where the tussocks of grass were dry. Sitting, staring up at the scaly branches, I thought I could feel the life of the great tree beating slowly through it, like the blood I heard in my own ears sometimes as I lay waiting for sleep. A dark shape flickered in over the valley walls and lit in a branch above my head. It was a bird, sky blue but touched at neck and wingtips with streaks of sunset red. It eyed me with such calm interest that I almost expected it to communicate with me as my mother did, in grunts or gestures.

We sat and watched each other, the bird and I, and slowly a strange idea began to creep over me: it was not the brightly coloured bird that examined me, but the old pine itself. Eyeless, it had summoned something with eyes so it could look at me, a stranger-thing, an intruder in its ancient domain. This odd thought brought another, even more frightening: handless, might it not summon something with curling fingers, grasping claws, to hold me until it decided what to do?

I stood up slowly. The bird only tipped its head to keep its bright eyes trained on mine. I backed away until I was out of the sun and the meadow became soft and swampy again beneath my feet, then I turned and clambered up the streambank towards the thorn hedge. The valley had gone quiet – no dragonflies, no wind sawing the grass; even the murmur of the water had grown more hushed. Keeping my pace slow and casual with that sense of something watching my back was the most difficult thing I had ever done. I could feel the bird's eye on me like a finger against my spine.

When I reached the thorn hedge, I turned. The valley still lay like a jewelled egg in a nest. The pine tree still loomed. The bright bird was gone.

As the fear ebbed, a kind of stubborn anger replaced it. This was *my* valley, I told myself. I had no words for that, but in a world where anything could be snatched from me at a moment's notice by my mother's gnarled brown fingers, the concept was as distinct as a single cloud in an empty sky. Mine. Even the tree, whatever it was, whatever it thought of me, was somehow mine. I would not be chased away. I would come back to this place whenever I wished.

I bobbed my head towards the ancient pine, a recognition of an equal rather than homage to a victor, then turned and made my painful, slow way back out beneath the brambles.

*

Do not speak, Miranda! I see by your look that you remember that place only too well. That you remember your . . . treachery. What other word is there? Even with all the serried ranks of noun and verb at my command, I can find no other way to describe what you did to me there. Stay! Stay! Here, feel: my hand is upon your neck — you must not struggle. I have not reached that part of the story yet. And you must hear it *all*.

But again I have raced ahead. There is time yet, more than enough time. Before you and your father came, before my mother's death, before even I reached the hidden valley, I was alive. If tonight is the only time my story is told, then I shall tell it in full.

The first thing I can remember is my mother bending low over the cook-fire, its glow playing across the sharp-edged face that sun and grime had darkened like old leather. How old was I? I will never know. It was an evening like many, many hundred others.

We lived in a hut of leaning sticks that she had built at the edge of the forest. A wide porch of sand stretched from the door down to the sea. I was amazed when I went back to see it, Miranda, after spending those years in the compound your father built — which *I* largely built, if the truth be told, acting as slave, labouring at his will. But when I returned to the place I had been born, and lived, I was astonished to see how small it was – scarcely larger than a shell for a man-sized crab. My mother and I had spent most of our time beneath the sky, and perhaps some idea of that greater and supremely vaulting roof overhead had coloured my memories. It was a dark cave, the house of my childhood, with a hole in the top to let some – but never enough – of the smoke float free.

My mother was mad, as I suppose I too am now mad. What else can people be who have seen their entire lives snatched away from them, and for no greater crime than being what they are? The choking, stifling unfairness of it is a permanent sore – one that can be lived with but never forgotten. Left to my mother's teachings and no other, though, I believe I would have been sane. In the universe that surrounded her, things simply *were*. To my childish eyes, she was unhappy in the same way that the day was hot or the tide was high. But your father, gagging on the injustices that had been done to him, taught me – along with the words that could describe such an alien thing in the first place – the cursed idea that there was such a thing as justice, as fairness, as right and wrong. Oh, wretched, cruel man!

Yes, in her own way, my mother was certainly mad. She sang to the storms, hunched in the shapeless black garments she had worn on her day of punishment and exile, and which were the only things she ever wore, however tattered and threadbare they became. She would squat outside the hut while I peered anxiously through the low doorway, and as the squall matted her grey-shot hair and soaked her ragged dress, she would bellow and moan to the sky. Only the rhythms – which still betimes float up into my thoughts unbidden – tell me that this was more than bestial anger or fear. As the wind howled and the lightning cracked, she sang. To my childish eyes, all three were equally powerful, equally frightsome.

Other times, such as on the night of my earliest memory, she sat and stared into the fire and dreamed for long, long hours, clucking and gurgling to herself. On some of those nights, her dreams swam into my head, murky visions of things I could not recognise, but which I feel sure were the places of her life before the island – flat, brown earth, mud houses, dry hills. And faces, angry and accusing. Imagine, Miranda: until you and Prospero came, the only human faces I saw, the only faces that peopled my dreams, were the ghosts out of my mother's bitter reveries.

All men are made by those who raise them, it is true, but was ever a man so crookedly shaped by two people, my mad mother and your cold father? They were the two opposites that swelled to fill my universe. Is it any wonder that I came to love you, Miranda? What else did I have? What else could I hope for?

*

One storm that I never saw myself, but experienced often in my mother's brooding dreams, must have happened soon after her landfall, while I was still nestled inside her belly. The vision of it came again and again, although it was only after she died that I came to understand its meaning. On that dreamt-of night the wind blew fiercely; the waves leaped high and sprays of pale foam leaped higher still. The great palm trees of the forest's edge bent nearly double. Then something fell burning from the sky.

It struck the beach in a mighty gout of flame, a fire bigger than anything my mother could have made if she had stacked dry timber for a week. A moment later, the blaze was only a crackle of red and amber light. Something rose from the pit it had dug into the sand, amorphous as smoke, but fast coalescing. My mother fought with it. I know not how she did, or why, but when her dreams of that night crept into me I could sense her fear, her anger, and even a taste of the cold satisfaction she felt when, after a long and nightmarish struggle, she at last found the chain of thought that would bind the thing. Nothing in her dream told me what had happened after that. Some great battle had been waged and I had been raised upon the empty battlefield, but I would never know its meaning, the truth of its resolution.

Or so I thought for a long time.

The HOLE

I HAD MY own battles. The island was bountiful, but not always kind.

Just as every branch seemed full of fruits so juice-swollen that they almost fell into my hand before I could pick them, life of other kinds thrived in equal measure: for every gaudy-feathered or sweetly singing bird there seemed a stinging insect of some kind – one of the reasons we lived with a hut full of smoke. These tiny armies were always at least a nuisance, but they were particularly vicious when twilight came. There were as many different types, it sometimes seemed, as there were grains of sand on the beach: hundred-legged worms, biting flies, green crawlers, jewel-shelled buzzers, flitterwings, scattersands, blanket-burrowers, each with its own determination and skills, each bent on piercing my young flesh. I quickly learned to wash the fruit-nectar from my face and hands when I had finished eating, for that drew them faster than anything: I also went about much of the time wearing a second skin of dried mud, which at least kept the shorter-toothed varieties at bay.

There were serpents on the island, too, and in nearly as great variety, from tiny thread-vipers scarcely the length of a finger to a single vast and luckily slow-moving python which lived in the trees on the island's far side – a beast ten paces long and as thick around as my waist, covered all over with a pattern of black and white and brown scales as intricate as any carpet in this great house of yours. I never let that old devil close enough to cause me any harm, but I often saw his glittering eye as he hung motionless from a branch, taking the sun and imperiously watching all that passed – especially a plump morselet like myself. He was in no hurry. For all I know he is back there on the island still, waiting. Perhaps he shall still get his chance with me some day.

One particular morning I was wandering on a hillside on the sunward side of the island. You may remember it, since the breadfruit trees grew there. This day was before you came, before my mother went gasping and thrashing to her death. It had been raining, and the ground and leaves were damp; even the air was wet. I was swishing along, kicking my feet in the tall grass to see the drops scatter, when I heard a rustling sound.

I dropped to my hands and knees, frightened, for whatever lurked in the undergrowth sounded quite large. I knew it was not my mother, for I had left her grinding roots on a flat stone before our hut only a short time earlier. Except for the great serpent, most of the animals that shared the island were smaller than me. There were a few timid deer and slot-eyed goats who seldom came down from the high places, at least by day. The monkeys who harboured in the deep forest were unafraid to roam by the sun's light, but they were none of them much taller than my knee, and also spent little time on the ground. Needless to say, I was both fearful of and fascinated by whatever might make such a commotion in the deep grasses.

As I lay peering, my chest and chin pressed against the sodden black earth, the stems leaned apart and a clutch of small pigs pushed out, snouts wrinkling as they whuffled with excitement. They were almost hairless, mottled grey and pink, and they gave no greater sign of alarm on seeing me than to change slightly the sound of their snorting. They inspected me for a long moment, then resumed nosing the earth, shoving and bumping each other when it seemed that one of them might have found something interesting. I watched, entranced. I may even have laughed. Then their mother appeared.

She was huge by any measure, a mountain of muscle and fat and coarse bristles, embellished with a red-shot eye. To a child lying on the ground at her feet she appeared an almost indescribable

monstrosity. If my mother had been capable of telling me tales of Satan and his demons, I promptly would have granted that sow a high seat in Hell's pantheon.

The only thing that saved me was sheer, terrified rabbiting. While she stared at me for an instant, then lowered her head, I sprang to my feet, took a step and a half to the nearest tree and leaped. If the tree had been a pace further, I would have died; of that I have no doubt. As it was, I caught only a glancing blow from her tusked mouth, but even so it tore a great furrow down my leg which I did not notice until I had climbed to the highest branch I could reach. When I finally saw the blood rushing out of me I nearly fell. I clutched the edges of ripped skin together and looked down. Grunting indignantly, the sow was circling the tree trunk, pausing from time to time to fix me with her malicious little eyes. The sight of her frightened me so badly that I almost lost my balance and tumbled, and I swear that she knew that. She moved to a spot just below me, waiting, but I only swayed for a moment before regaining my footing on the blood-slicked branch.

Wordless though I was, still I knew that there were certain things I should do – my mother had tied me and patched me after enough mishaps. I went always naked in those days except for armouring mud, so there was nothing from which to make a bandage. The tree itself had not leaves but needles. There was nothing I could do to staunch my bleeding except hold the flaps of my gashed leg together with my fingers.

And the sow would not go. The piglets seemed perfectly content to mill about in the clearing beneath the tree, digging with their tiny snouts and squealing at one another, so there was nothing to draw the mother away. A dragging hour went past and still they would not leave. The small creatures that had so charmed me only a short while earlier now seemed demons tormenting me on purpose. How I cursed them, even as I soaked the ground with tears and blood, but to no avail. The piglets gambolled, then slept in the tree's shade, bellies puffing in and out. The mother watched me with an eye red as my wound, cold as a river stone. The day wore on and I clung to the branch, dizzy, weak, and increasingly certain that nothing could save me.

I shouted for my own mother, of course – I shrieked until my voice was a ragged wheeze – but here I had invited my own misfortune: Sycorax had become used to my roving, if not reconciled. I might get a beating on my return, but she had long since stopped searching for me, since she knew I had found hiding places she could not reach. I made the clearing echo with my wordless wailing, bellowed until it seemed I must shake the sky off its fundamental pillars, but no one came.

The sun moved higher in the sky overhead, turning the grey sky warm and bright, steaming the last moisture from the earth and vegetation – but not before I had licked up every standing drop of rain within my reach.

As the day grew hotter I became weaker and more light-headed, until it seemed I might just float off the branch like a scrap of ash and be carried away over the rough hills. Once I thought I felt my spirit slip from my body and fly to the beach where my mother squatted, frying cakes on a hot stone beside the fire; but if I truly went there, she was not aware of my spirit-self, of my need. Her back remained bent, her face turned away from me as she slapped the root paste into sticky balls. In my desperate state I may only have dreamed that my spirit departed my body – certainly the sight of my mother making root cakes was something I knew very well. In any case, she did not come. The day grew stiflingly hot. I dipped in and out of sleep. The pain and fright would become less for a moment, and I would let myself slide down into the feeling as though into cool water. A moment later I would awake in heart-speeding terror as I felt myself beginning to pitch forward. And the sow would still be looking up, staring, waiting . . .

And then she departed. With no warning, long before the sun touched the western horizon, she suddenly gave an angry grunt and went crashing off into the grass. Her piglets formed an untidy company and bobbled after her, tripping one another in their haste to keep up. She was finally gone . . . or was she? My horrible thirst and the throbbing, wrenching ache of my leg had nearly overpowered me, but my fear of the beast was greater. I waited no little time before beginning my climb down.

The journey to the bottom was excruciating. Even my good leg was painfully stiff; the agony of the other is something I can only leave you to imagine. And the climb set the wound to pumping again. I tried to run for the first few steps, in case the sow should return, but it was useless – I could barely walk. I fell down several times on my journey back to the beach. On the last occasion I almost did not get up, so powerful was the urge to sleep, to slip into gentle blackness.

I made my way back just after dark. It was one of the few times I saw my mother Sycorax frightened. Even as she raised her hand to slap me, she saw my leg, covered foot to thigh in blood, both dried and sticky-new. Her eyes bulged, and she gave out a gurgling cry of terror that I barely even heard.

She was unusually kind after she had cleaned the wound, covered it with root leaf poultices, and tied my leg tight with a strip of cloth torn from her own and only garment. She took me into the hut and cradled my head in her lap as she poured some hot liquid down my throat, then hummed wordlessly to me as I sank into the dark.

You are wondering why I tell you this story, Miranda – I can see it in your face. And at the same moment you are hoping that I have wandered so far in the field of my memories that I am now babbling, that I do not realise how the time is flying away. Not so, my inconstant friend. I know when the next guards will come, and how long after that until old Somnambulo is missed. And everything I tell you is for a reason. My speech is hot, but my heart and blood are cold, cold, cold.

You see, that was the time I learned about hatred. As I shook with the fever that followed, as I lay retching up the thin broths my mother fed me, as I writhed with the pain of the healing wound, I came to hate the creature that had done this to me.

At first I felt only fear. I thought I saw the sow's evil little eyes gleaming in the shadows when I could not sleep, and her hot, stinking breath seemed to follow me into my dreams. But after a while, as the horrid event itself was partially covered by the collecting pile of days, I began to concentrate instead on the injury done me, and the fear turned to black hatred. When I could stand at last, and found myself a cripple, barely able to hop from one end of our stretch of beach to the other, confined by my infirmity to a stranglingly small patch of land – and to the permanent presence of my mother, whose solicitude had long since vanished – the hatred began to curdle into something cooler and more calculating. I began to ponder revenge.

Long after the sow had surely forgotten me, I

thought of her and wished her ill. Perhaps this is an example of what your father told you so many times: that I was and am no better than a beast myself. I wonder. In any case, I had been wronged, and could not forget. I would return pain for pain . . . at least.

I learned to hate. I learned to take a wrong and treasure it like a tiny spark on a cold, wet evening. Each time that the passage of days or the improvement of my health came near to extinguishing the spark, I held it close and blew on it until it flamed again. I nurtured the heat. I held it close to me, although sometimes it was an exhausting task.

Never underestimate how much work there is in hatred, Miranda.

When I could walk well enough to leave the confines of my mother's domain again, I made my way back to the hillside where I had been so unfairly attacked. I carried a sharp, fire-hardened sick which gave me at least a small sense of protection, although in truth I think it would have been of little more use than fingernails and teeth against that huge creature. Nevertheless, in some obscure way I felt better with it grasped in my hand. I had made the spear some seasons before, and had used it from time to time to poke rather uselessly at the bright fish that sheltered among the rocks in the ocean shallows. At least the sow would be a larger and less elusive target.

So, my heart pounding and rattling in my breast, I returned to the place where Death's wing had brushed me. But for the hoofprints of the sow and her young in the mud, there was no sign of my nemesis. I knelt on the spot where they had first crossed the clearing before me and began to dig. A gob of mud came up in my cupped hands. I tossed it aside and gouged again.

It was not the work of a single day, although I had emptied a great trough in the wet soil by the time the sun began to sink. Muddy and exhausted, my leg aching so that the walk back was only slightly easier than on the day the sow had torn it, I returned to my mother's silent company. After eating I fell asleep quickly, and was back in my pit before the sun was above the hilltop the next morning.

Towards the middle of the day I stopped to drink some of the water which had collected in a hollow of stone. After I drank, I surveyed what I had made, the gouge in the earth that was now deeper than I was tall, a black hole, empty but for the wide tree branch propped against the side to help me climb in and out. Thin tendrils of root protruded from the torn soil, white and shocked. The sight made me uncomfortable.

There was something *wrong* with the hole; I could feel that, but I could not discern what it was. I puzzled for a long time, so long that the mud that coated me dried to a scaly crust. No matter how I paced about the hole's rim or squinted at its steep sides, I could see nothing. It was a pit, a place in which to trap the creature which had tried to kill me.

It was made exactly as it should be made. Why did the sight of it disturb me so?

Shrugging, I clambered back down into the hole and resumed my labours.

When the sun fell behind the pit's deepening side, the muddy earth became abruptly colder. I looked up, and although the sky was still the same cloudy blue, the darkness of the hole felt oppressive. I decided that I had dug deep enough.

I had a moment of fear when the branch I used for climbing slipped a little on the pit's damp wall and I almost fell back down, but enough of my upper body was balanced on the rim to pull myself out. I turned and pulled the branch up after me, then spent the rest of the diminishing afternoon covering the hole, first with a mat woven of long, flexible branches, then with sod and leaves. When I was finished, it was almost impossible to detect that this patch of ground was different from any other part of the hillside. My mother never ventured so far from the hut any more, and something as light as a monkey or the island's small deer would not break the screen of branches; only my enemy would find herself the victim of my diligent hatred. So why was I still troubled?

My understanding tried beyond its undeveloped powers, I returned to the beach.

I did not sleep well that night, but lay long past moonrise with my hands behind my head, staring up into the dim shadowy corners of the hut, listening with growing unrest to my mother's harsh snoring. When I did fall asleep I tumbled into a deeper darkness full of staring eyes, squealing, shrieking voices, and the scent of blood.

A curious shakiness was on me when I awoke. I loitered about the camp all morning, strangely unwilling to go and check my trap. But at last my mother cuffed me for some minor irritation and I stamped off into the forest.

It took me no little time to make my way up to that place on the hillside where I had spent so much of the previous days. I found a dozen things to catch my attention: monkeys playing games in the high branches of a fruit tree; a newborn butterfly with wings each as wide as my hand, drying itself in the sun; a new dam of sticks forming in one of the streams birthed in the mountain's highland – virtually everything I saw seemed more interesting than the pit. But at last I reached the spot where I had laboured so long, and saw immediately that my efforts had been successful.

The branches that had screened the trap were a shattered ruin. The dirt and leaves that had hidden them had fallen away, so that the hole gaped as nakedly as when I had first finished digging. And something was grunting angrily in the depths of the earth.

I crept to the edge, more than half-convinced that my enemy, if it was indeed she, might be spurred by the sight of me to leap all the way out. I knew little or nothing of pigs, and just enough of her cruel strength to consider anything possible.

She did indeed give a great honking cry when I peered over the rim, and charged the pit's walls, but the soil only crumbled beneath her flailing trotters. I shied away, but after a few moments regained my courage and moved back to where I could look down on what I had accomplished.

Years later I saw in one of your father's books a picture of a demon immured in Hell. The artist had done his best to show both the monstrousness of its evil and the hopeless anguish of the damned soul festering within it. Until that moment I had been delighted with the engravings, charmed by the art that could make a representation at once so flat and so intricate, but when I saw that demon's image I went cold and shut the book. I had seen that look before.

The sow was hunkered down at the bottom of the pit, so covered in mud that she seemed almost an excrescence of the troubled earth. Her eyes gleamed wickedly out of the blackness, and when she saw me again she bellowed her anger, her tusked yawp a great vibrating red gouge. Her stinking breath floated up in a cloud.

But she was trapped, and it showed in her every movement, sounded in her cries: all her strength and ferocity could do nothing. She was helpless. What she could reach she could seize and rend and destroy, but she could not fight her own bulk or the unresisting soil which only fell away beneath her scrabbling feet. Because she could not understand, she could not escape.

I was both delighted and horrified to see that in her miserable fury she had rasped at her own legs, so that they were as coated with dirt-caked blood as my own had been. I had won. Still, there was something about the immensity of her suffering that left me feeling curiously empty. I stared for a while at the damned, furious eyes, then stood and walked away down the hillside.

I do not know how long I wandered, but I found myself at last in front of the thorn hedge that guarded my secret valley. I made my way beneath the brambles and walked down through the damp meadow to the base of the great pine tree, which this time gave off no feeling of menace or challenge, but rather seemed somehow welcoming. I sat, leaning against the rough bark, and stared up through the green lacework of needles, dizzying myself with the height of the trunk that stretched up above me.

While I walked my thoughts had been flittering in all directions inside my head, aimless and unhelpful as flies. The hatred that had spurred me was now hard to remember. I had a dim sense of the sow, of her angry fearfulness, and that in turn had reminded me of the look on my mother's face when I had returned with my wounded leg. Had not the sow been protecting her own children as my mother would have protected me? Should she be punished for that? During the planning of my revenge I had thought once of luring her piglets to me and killing them before her eyes, the worst revenge against a mother I could – or for that matter, can now – imagine. I could no longer bear the thought. What crime could warrant such a terrible, terrible punishment?

What crime, Miranda? Surely nothing so simple as what the sow had done.

Now I could not imagine inflicting any more punishment on her at all. She was terrified and trapped. Surely that was enough. In truth, the taste of my victory was far less sweet than I had imagined.

I considered how I might set her free, should I choose to do so. I was not so foolish as to imagine she would be grateful, so any method of release had to encompass my own safety. Perhaps, I thought, I could balance a large log beside the edge of the pit and then tip it over with my spear from the safety of a tree branch, allowing her to climb out . . .

But even as I played with these thoughts, and enjoyed the warm sensation of magnanimity that suffused me like a golden mist, something else began to creep into my mind.

At first it was hardly notable, merely a sullen irritation that I should contemplate giving the author of my injuries the reprieve she would never have given to me. But then, as I leaned against the tree and watched its branches blowing back and forth, slowly swaying, the feeling became stronger. I experienced again, as strongly as when it had first happened, the pain of my leg and my terror that I would die. How could I so quickly forget what she had done to me? Again I saw the face of the trapped sow in my mind's eye, but this time her rage had nothing of fright in it, only pure malignity.

The thoughts of mercy I had been harbouring suddenly seemed weak; I pushed back against the tree trunk and felt strength flowing into me, angry strength, as though the vitality of the old pine passed through its bark and into my blood. It was almost as if the ancient tree itself was stiffening my resolve, helping me turn away from my earlier, laughable weakness.

Only a few more moments passed before I leapt to my feet and clambered back up the meadow to the thorn hedge. I hurried back toward my trap.

It did not take me long to find a boulder which, with only a little digging, I could free from the muddy hillside's embrace. Rolling it down toward the pit, bracing it with sticks to keep it moving in the direction I wished, I felt an almost supernatural control and power. The sow began squealing again as she heard my approach, a terrible ragged sound that made me want to put my fingers in my ears. Instead I leaned my shoulder against the poised stone and pushed with all my might, feet slipping and then finally digging in. The boulder rocked, then the rim collapsed and it toppled over.

There was a terrible wet thump, then a long train of bubbling gasps trailed at last by silence.

Later, I took some of the blood and returned to the valley, where I daubed it on the old pine tree's trunk. Then, all feelings of victory replaced by exhausted emptiness, I returned to the hut and slept a long, black, and dreamless sleep.

Ah. You did not know about the sow, did you, Miranda? I never told you. I think I was ashamed. But tonight – ah, what is the night your folk wear masks and then take them off again? Midsummer's Eve? Tonight the hidden faces will be seen.

Human faces can be masks, too, although I did not understand that for most of my young life. The idea of hiding thoughts behind an unrevealing expression was something I learned from Prospero, who showed almost nothing to the world. Even slower to come was the conception of placing a mask over someone else's face – of seeing in them only what one wishes to see.

I wonder what you first thought when you saw me staring down from the rocks on the day of your arrival. *I* had eyes mostly for your dreadful, fascinating father, who my alarmed senses told me was by far the greater threat – although now I am not so sure that was true. You were only an appurtenance . . . then. It was later I would come to understand what your name meant.

But what did *you* see crouching on the rock before you? A huddled brown thing with yellow eyes that stared, stared, as a baby bird gawps from its nest? An unfurred monkey, lithe and long-armed? Or an ill-made doll, like a poor copy formed from mud of some toy from your lost childhood? Was that your thought when you first saw me, sad Miranda? That all your toys would now be like this, poor and unsatisfactory?

I know what your father thought when he saw me, for as I scuttled back down the rock, seeking shelter from his awful gaze, he told me — or rather, told you. Although I could not then understand his words, he reminded me of them later, when I spoke your tongue. On that day I listened for only a few moments before terror overcame me and I fled.

Look, Miranda, he said. His voice was as coldly interested as if he had found me lying dead and decayed upon the sand. *This apparently deserted island seems to have at least a few larger inhabitants. An ape, I think — no, perhaps something a shade more interesting. A so-called 'natural man' — a savage. A cannibal.*

And as I ran, Miranda, I heard your small, puzzled voice.

Calibal . . . ?

I was frightened on the day of your coming, and knew it. I was less aware of how lonely I was.

My mother died suddenly, as you know. She was

greedy of her food, and, free of the need to speak or even listen, let nothing interrupt her when she was filling her mouth . . . but as I learned from hard experience, she still could communicate perfectly well in her own way, even while chewing. Many times I was sent away with my ears ringing and my eyes full of tears when I tried to pull a little more flesh from the bone she was holding.

Despite the abundance of fruit and green things on our island, or perhaps because of it, as I grew I craved meat of all kinds. Fish we had, but never in abundance, and my mother's snares never captured enough birds or other small game to satisfy me. When some small carcass was roasting over the flames, the scent of it drew me like a magical spell. I would drink the odour with my nose, pushing my face all the way into the smoke until I coughed so hard I hurt myself.

It might seem a wonder, then, that I never tried to bring back any of that dead pig, or even tasted its flesh. In fact, one smear of its hot blood on my tongue had set me gagging. I covered the carcass over with dirt and tried not to think about it – with little success, as you might guess. The solitary mind probes at an ugly thought as at a wound, constantly seeing if the pain is less, and by so doing keeps it alive beyond its time.

Flesh to eat was in short supply, so it was no surprise that betimes my mother and I should almost come to blows when there was but one fishy skeleton between us and she insisted on mumbling the last bits of flesh from the bones: as I grew larger than she, I more and more thought it unfair that she should have such a privilege. It was on just such an occasion that she raised a bony hand to cuff me away, then suddenly stopped.

At first I thought that she was trying to conjure up some new noise, a sound so ambitious and unprecedented that its generation required an enormous struggle. She rocked back and forth, waving her flexing fingers as though they were burnt, then staggered onto her feet. Her face contorted into an astonishing succession of masks, then began to turn dark, as though some internal light flickered and failed. She reeled, clutching at her throat, and fell.

What did I do? I stood and watched, of course, and remained standing for long moments after she had dropped to the ground. I had no comprehension of what had happened. At first I thought she had fallen asleep, overwhelmed by the attempt to trumpet out this new sound. When after a short time she had not moved again, I went and touched her gently, for on the few occasions of fatigue or illness when she had slept later than I, she had proved rather unpleasantly that she did not enjoy being awakened.

But she did not wake this time, nor did she move again. Slowly, wretchedly, I began to perceive the truth. Just as quickly as that, I was alone. The only other person I knew, the only other human creature in my life, was gone.

No, it was worse than that, if such a thing is possible. Not only my sole companion but my only god had died. That is something no one but me can ever understand — the utter loneliness, the abandonment, the sudden and shatteringly fearful emptiness of my universe. That night, terrified, I dragged my mother's body to the hut. Already she had grown cold, but I wrapped us both in my mat of soft reeds and held her until dawn, trying to bring back the warmth. Surely, ran my wordless and confused thoughts, it was only a longer sleep, a deeper sleep. Surely in the morning I would feel her bony fingers tugging on my ear to awaken me. It would be just like any other day, and the previous night would pass into my memory as merely one more of my mother's oddities. I lay trembling, cradling a corpse, and strove to re-weave the fabric of reality by force of will.

But when I awoke she was cold and unmoving, though her eyes were still open. When I touched her, searching for the reassuring throb of the vein in her neck, a drumbeat that had lulled me to sleep throughout my infancy, I felt instead the horrid distention of her throat, the fatal shape of the bone lodged there.

Much of what happened next is lost to me. I know that I stumbled up and down the beach keening at the sky, which did not seem to know that the world had ended. I know that I ran in the forest until my feet and hands and face were bloodied by rocks and whipping branches. I seem to remember spending an entire night shivering, submerged to my neck in a stream – but it is all a smear of sound and vision, of alternating light and shadow. It might have been days that I lived in madness.

At last I returned to my home. My mother was still there, although the passage of time had drawn her body into a strange posture, bending her double as though she struggled to sit up; her lips had pulled back from her broken teeth. She might have been crying for me, or laughing at my foolishness. I could not bear to look at her, but neither could I think of what to do. For another few days I lived on the beach and avoided the camp, going through the motions of life – eating, sleeping, fetching water from the stream – circling at a great distance around my mother's remains, but unable to so easily avoid the gaping emptiness that had been her centrality, her omnipresence, her . . . *mother*-ness. But I sensed that I could not go on that way forever: even an animal, which was what I was at that moment, knows when it is injured it must heal itself. Something had to be done so that I could live again.

And even worse, she was beginning to stink.

Hoping for some clarity, some contemplative stillness far from the horror of our camp, I at last made my way to the valley and the shadow of the ancient pine, but this time the presence of the tree brought me no stiffening of my resolution. Instead, I seemed almost to sense the spirit of the thing gloating, as though something long hoped-for had occurred. It made me queasy, and I swiftly quit the valley once more.

The only thing I could think of was the sow, down in the hole, and how it had eased me somewhat to cover her with dirt. Thus, I spent the remainder of that afternoonn digging a similar pit for my mother. Experience had taught me that the sea's relentless fumbling soon exposed any bones of fish or fowl we buried on the beach, so I made Sycorax's grave at the edge of the forest, digging with my hands until my fingers bled and the sweat drizzled from me like rain. When I had finished, I wrapped her in the mat so I could carry her, then tumbled her noisome body down into the depths – the memory makes me shudder even now! – and quickly covered it over.

I knew no prayers, obviously; I did not even know that such things existed. If my mother worshipped Setebos, as your father claimed, she went to him unshriven. I knew nothing of what the dead might want. I was myself just another empty hole.

Two Dancing PUPPETS

Hᴏᴡ ᴄᴀɴ I make you understand what I felt when my mother died? Your own mother died at your birth; you did not know her. And with all the suffering of your solitude, you always had Prospero your father, the foundation on which your life was erected. Also, even in your island exile you knew there were other people in the world, some who had been kind to you, even loved you. But I had only that mad old woman, and when she was taken from me by a fishbone I had less than nothing, for I could not conceive of there being anything else remotely like me. The island *was* my world, and I knew as no other person knows that the world was empty of human company.

As if to prove your father's assertions of my bestiality, I did survive. Despite the howling emptiness, the speechless grief, the madness of my solitude, I lived. I do not know why. Life is a tenacious thing, Miranda. You have seen a fish flopping on stone, an impossible distance from water but still squirming and struggling towards redemption. That irreducible atom of life within us all is fierce. Ah, *there* is a miracle greater than any other your God is deemed to have performed: that something inside us should live, and living should struggle against the inevitability of death.

So, just as my mother had spent her last moments trying uselessly to disgorge the bone, I strove to keep myself among the living as well. Perhaps if I had received the benefits of civilisation I might have conceived the idea that dying myself I might join my mother and end my loneliness. But in truth I did not perceive that the thing that had happened to her might happen to me as well. How could the world end? When I was frightened, as when the sow attacked me, I was afraid of painful injury, of being separated somehow from my mother and the things I knew, but the idea of a final ending did not – could not – occur to me, let alone an ending that I could effect.

And even if such an idea had come, I do not know that I could have accomplished it. As I said, Miranda, the spark of life, that monad or divine breath or whatever it might be, is fierce. It is stubborn even in the face of indescribable horror, and I am the living proof. Has ever a creature been as cruelly deserted as I? And not once, but twice?

*

Your father considered me little more than an animal, and that is the way he lured me, with food and soft words. It did not take him long to find my hut, and that is where he made your first camp. Even then, in my ignorance, I sensed that there was something dangerous about a creature who would so blithely occupy another's territory, but I still cannot understand his thought. Could he, who himself had been driven from Milan by a usurper, not see that he did the same? Or was his talk of justice always deceitful? Perhaps he knew on that very first day that he would take me and tame me, then use me. Certainly my mother's hut was only the first of the many things he stole from Caliban.

I should have run! I should have fled to the far side of the island, or into the hills. Neither you nor your father, with your city-soft muscles, could have followed me there! I could have stayed free a long time, perhaps forever. But I was lonely, Miranda. Twice since my mother's death a dusting of snow had come to the high peaks and the days had shrunk to their shortest duration. Two years of solitude had passed before your boat grounded upon my island. I was lonely.

So he lured me. He put sweetmeats on a flat leaf and placed them in the shade at the forest's edge so that I could take them without needing to approach too closely. There he failed, because those dainty things — concoctions of honey, nuts, and spices carefully packed for you by some snuffling cook, some obedient-in-the-blood house-slave — those little civilised trifles which had come so far across the water smelled nothing like food to me at all. They were muskily unfamiliar, as unappetising as stones dipped in strong perfume would be to you. I would not take them, not even touch them. But even as I grimaced from my leafy retreat at those strange offerings, the smells of fish wafting over from your camp . . . or once even a roasting deer, crackling in its fat . . . tormented me.

When he saw I did not accept the sweetmeats, Prospero tried other things. Mangoes and pears and pomegranates, the largest and most succulent he could find, he left for me on a rock in the shade at the edge of the trees. But I could find fruit any time I wished; even in my wretched orphanhood, I was not ready to sell myself so cheaply.

And even as I played at my disinterest, even as I searched for and discovered a hundred little omens, a thousand unvoiced superstitions against taking your father's gifts, I was fascinated by the new arrivals. I dimly sensed that you might somehow be creatures like myself — although my total experience of humankind had only swelled from two to four — but I was not entirely sure. Where my mother had perpetually worn her shapeless frock of flapping black, and I myself wore nothing, you and your father seemed to change constantly. When first I saw you, little Miranda, you wore the rags of your castle finery; other days, your father let you run along the edge of the surf wearing little more than a thin shift stuck to your small, cubbish body by the wet spray. And Prospero sometimes doffed his black robes to reveal beneath them breeches and shirt of startingly colourful design. Once I even saw him strip to the waist to dig a trench; the tufts of hair on his chest were as ash-grey as his beard. Changing, changing, changing: like birds or snakes, you moulted and then renewed yourselves with astonishing frequency.

In the end, a bit of roasted fish proved my undoing.

Gutted and cooked over a low fire, then set out on a platter of leaves, it had a magical lure quite different from the sweets or fruit. I crouched in the greenery and stared at it for a long time, until all the world seemed to drop away and the universe contained only me and that glaze-eyed, black and silver-scaled object. My nostrils widened; I could feel them spreading, greedy for the tangy scent.

I looked around, but the trap was far too subtle for my primitive understanding. You and your father were walking on the beach, far away, your backs towards me. I could see you circling around him like a hummingbird visiting and revisiting a flower. If you were there, you could not be here. Therefore, it would be safe to take the fish.

Still I struggled, unable to understand why I resisted, but sensing somehow that if I accepted that gloriously alluring gift, things would . . . change.

Oddly, I thought of the hidden valley and the ancient tree, which I had visited only a few times since my mother's death. Perhaps because I had kept it secret from my mother, after she died I had come to associate the place with a dim sense of unease – a little like what I felt about the murdered sow. Still, I was drawn there as I was drawn to the fish lying before me, and both things filled me with what in retrospect I see as a sort of shamed desire.

Thinking of the tall old tree and secret valley helped me make up my mind . . . but not in the right way. The valley had brought me no true harm, I told myself – not in words, Miranda, no: my internal discussions were more like rainstorms of feeling pushed about by contrary winds – and it had brought me much in the way of sanctuary and strange, new, often pleasurable feelings. The valley had not harmed me – was I not still free to go where I wished and do what I chose? So how could a simple piece of fish, from however alien a hand, be anything but what it seemed to be?

I took it, a sudden grab, and retreated into the forest, heart hammering.

It was delicious, of course. Flaky and juicy, with not a bone anywhere between tail and head. How your father managed that – well, he was a sorcerer, was he not? Subtle snares require subtle sorceries. He was capable of greater ones, as I found out before too long.

The next day I found another fish on the shaded

rock. Again you and your father were in plain sight, a good distance away. Taking it was much easier the second time.

What did you think, Miranda, as your father slowly drew in the net? Did you think he was finding you a playfellow? Or trapping some oddly human but still particularly toothsome morsel for you to swallow and digest, just as he caught deer and rabbits and fish? Did you glimpse for a moment the fact that he was doing both?

After enough bits of cooked flesh had disappeared down my gullet, I began to loiter around the outskirts of the camp, in plain view, but ready at any moment to bolt. Ah, but your father was sly. I suppose a man who can summon and control demons is well versed in patient manipulation.

He began to look at me – nothing more. From halfway across the beach he would stand and regard me. I would stare into those glacial blue eyes of his for long moments, watching for anything that looked like hostile intent, prepared to spring away at any moment. Though Prospero fascinated me, I thought I was still looking over the walls of my separateness at an invader. I did not realise that he was already inside the citadel. Where once I had seen the faces of my mother's bitter dreams, now my sleep was haunted by that one face: cold, knowing eyes, thin half-smiling lips, a brow like the rocks on the headland.

One morning, when the sun was still only a glow behind the eastern hills, he came to the edge of the forest. He sat on the ground with his back to the trees and waited. I ventured closer, soundless as a caterpillar, but he knew I was there.

Slowly, with a calmness meant to soothe my animal fears, he began to move his hands before him. Intrigued, but blocked by the long thin shape of his back, I eased along the forest fringe until I could see what he was doing. With a bowl full of water he was moistening the fine dirt; as I watched, he began to form the mud into small round shapes.

Ah, your father's hands, his long, capable fingers! I watched them open-mouthed as they squeezed and patted, smoothed and shaped with a dexterity I could not understand, so different was it from my mother's crabbed twitching. Even years later I remained amazed by your father's hands; that day, the first time I had ever seen their busy capability up close, I was enthralled.

He found a slender stick and began breaking it into pieces. At the first crack I shied, but Prospero did not look up. I held my ground as he began to wrap his rolls of clay around the twigs, his fingers sliding so quickly and gracefully that for long moments I watched them rather than the things they were shaping . . . but before long it was impossible to ignore what was taking form. He had made a little doll, a manikin which could lie on its back in his cupped hand. He set it down and then made another, slightly smaller. When this was done, your father took a few drops of water from the bowl and flicked them at the two figures with whipcrack fingers, then reached into his robe; when he took his hand out again and fluttered it over the little dolls' heads, a dusting of brilliant yellow and blue sifted down. Strangely, even to my untutored eye, all the blue dust stuck to one figure's head, but the yellow adhered to the top of the smaller.

Still not raising his eyes, though I was so fascinated I might not have bolted even had he lurched towards me, your father lifted them up, held them close to his mouth, and breathed on them in turn as he spoke their names.

Arlecchino, he said. Then: *Columbina*.

As he spoke, first the blue-headed figure, then the golden, squirmed in his hands.

I must have let out a gasp, for he smiled deep in his beard, but still did not turn toward me. Mind you, I was not civilised: to me this trick was no more magical than catching a hidden fish in a deep pool or picking a leaf that made soup taste good. But unlike those other useful things, both of which I had seen my mother do, this was new to me. And even though I did not understand that this was *magic* – that back in Milan he might have been denounced to the church and burned in public for this harmless display – I was still delighted.

Dance, Arlecchino, he said. Words and names alike meant nothing to me then, but I saw him perform this conjuration on other occasions – and once a similar but unpleasantly different version.

Arlecchino, the faceless mud-man, bowed, then began to dance. Slowly and carefully at first, as though he did not know himself whether his gelid legs could hold him, or whether his tree-twig bones might not snap, the little doll began to caper.

Dance, Columbina, whispered your father, and the golden-headed figure joined her mate.

Prospero then slowly stood, but instead of moving any closer, he turned on his heel and walked away down the slope and onto the beach. The rush of the sea was in my ears and for a moment I forgot the two manikins to watch him go. He did not look back. He seemed impossibly tall.

Arlecchino and his Columbina whirled and cavorted. I crept nearer, lowering myself until my face was at the level of their dance, but they were less frightened of me than I of them. Their sticky, nub-handed arms met and they twirled about each other. Arlecchino lifted Columbina and tossed her in the air, then caught her as she fell, although he stumbled for a moment and one of his legs lost a bit of clay. They went on that way for some time, then gradually slowed. At last, as if by mutual assent, they lay down side by side and stopped moving.

A tear ran down my cheek. I slid closer and carefully lifted the little golden-headed doll in my hand. Her clay was cool to the touch, and there was no sign whatsoever of the force that had animated her. Arlecchino was similarly inert. Respectfully, anxiously, I set them down again. Had I killed them somehow? But I had done nothing but watch. Should they be buried in the ground, even though they were already made of earth? It was all too much for me. I retreated to the forest and walked for some time in its depths, trying to herd my thoughts when they wished to run untrammelled.

It was not long before I would take food from Prospero's hand. Certainly, I would snatch it and snarl as I backed away, warning him not to presume on my condescension . . . but I was his. He owned me, as surely as ever a man has owned his dog or his horse. How you giggled, Miranda, to see me growling. Since you were accustomed to your father's cleverness, I imagine you considered me just one more of his tricks. How entertaining of him, to find you an amusement like this, a little creature almost human, almost animal, and not quite enough of either.

When the glare of your father's regard did not blind me completely, I could see you, too, Miranda. You were one of the things that had begun to lure me in closer. You were my size, for a start — a little smaller, if anything. And where I stalked and skulked and crept about, hackles a-ruffle, you went boldly. Your confidence dazzled me. Did you have power over snakes, I wondered, since you did not seem to fear their bites? All I could see was that you wandered as you wished with scarcely a look down to see what might lie at your feet.

I cannot say you were beautiful. I am certain that you were, but I had no point of comparison. All I can remember is that I thought you almost as strange as your father, but far less frightening. He was a storm at sea. You were sunlight glancing on the waves.

Even then your hair was long, dangling below your rump as you stood pondering an oddly shaped insect, flying behind you like a lyrebird's tail when you ran. I cannot quite make out the colour now, by candlelight, but where it spreads on your pillow there it seems no different, a luminous brown with coppery streaks. My mother was dark. I was dark – see, even the hair on my arms is as black as a beetle's case. Your father's black was shot through with drear grey and white. And there were you, with hair like autumn, like fire, like the colour of hope. I did not know what to make of you.

You have always had a sombre gaze, Miranda. When I sidled to the edge of the camp, you would regard me solemnly, as though I were something very important. Can you wonder I came to love you? Then, a moment later, your eyes would crease closed and a great whoop of laughter would escape. Later on, I learned to make it happen. Oh, that was a glorious day, the first time I ever purposefully made you laugh!

And what did I look like? I am a monster now – perhaps in part because the hatred that burns within has melted me like candle-wax. When I tried to move about Milan in daylight, those who did not simply shrink from me stared and whispered among themselves. But in those long-ago days, before your father's evil treatment and your betrayal had soured me, what shape did I wear?

Prospero told you that I was fathered on Sycorax by a demon. Perhaps he was right – he mentioned it as off-handedly as when he noted that the day would be cloudy. That was indeed part of the tale told of my mother's banishment, nor do I know who my father truly was. I never saw him in my mother's dreams, or at least I saw no generative act that would have separated his face from the rest of that choir of unpleasant ghosts. But whoever or whatever he might have been to my mother, he was not a pretty young suitor. When I first saw that Ferdinand, whose name still sours in my mouth when I speak it, it was clear that he and the other shipwrecked mariners shared something with you that I did not. Tall, they all were tall, even the old, bent ones. None of them had my long arms, my low brow. None of them had eyes like mine. I have never seen anyone with eyes like mine.

Your father called me 'Cannibal', but he also called me 'Ape', and 'Demonspawn' when he was angry. 'Little savage' when he was in a kinder mood. But never 'Son'. No one has ever called me that.

And you could never quite decide whether I was 'Caniban' or 'Calibal', until the smear of use and your father's amused endorsement gave me my name.

But what did I look like? Did you see the heart of me, Miranda, the thing that burned inside me that did not know it was a brute? No, say nothing. You are not the child you were then. Time and words have corrupted you as well. You are no longer to be trusted.

A breath, a pause, a thought. For such a long-awaited night, these hours fly fast. So much to tell!

A parent's love is a strange, strong thing. I am confused about it still; I was even less certain then. The more I was dazzled by the attention of Prospero, the more I came to pine for the simpler attentions of my mother. Yes, she had smacked at me and then clung to me in irritating alternation, but those times when I was small and she held me in her arms were the only moments of real peace I can remember. When the storms grew frighteningly loud outside our hut, I would crawl through the dark towards her, searching with my hands until I found the bony curve of her breast rising and falling. Half-awakened, she would wrap her arms around me and draw me close, cradling my head in the hollow of her neck. The distinct and unique combination of odours that was my mother's scent would surround me and I would feel the fear slide away. Sometimes before she fell back into sleep she would even sing to me, so quietly that I could just hear her mumbling croon through the voice of the wind.

Though she was mad, my mother's wishes seem clear enough. She wanted my love, or at least my companionship. She wanted my help when she grew old and could not do for herself. I do not think she was without wishes for my happiness, but she had done everything that could be done in that way: she had taught me to survive, she had fed me and raised me. She could not find me companions or a mate, and could only ease my loneliness with her own presence. I wonder whether she would have done anything differently had she known how soon I would be left completely alone?

But Prospero's goals I still do not understand. He tamed me, yes, like a dog that he needed to guard his campfire. But if all he wanted was a cur, why did he teach me to speak, and even to read a little? If he needed me to understand him so that I could be a better slave, why point out the stars to me? Was he interested in the limits of my half-humanity? Was I another experiment, like the alchemical ponderings that had so captured his interest in Milan that he was oblivious to his brother's plotting?

By the middle of the first year after your arrival, I was coming to the camp each day as though it were my home again, although I was still too skittish to sleep within reach of what were still frighteningly unknowable strangers. And each day, as Prospero drew me further into his web with food and small kindnesses, he threw me scraps of learning with the bits of meat.

I had come to understand that 'Miranda' was a sound that was particularly you, although the concept of a name was a little longer in coming. I did not know it, but with the first word I learned Latin as well as Milanese, for you were indeed something admirable, something to be wondered at. Although I was shy, I was besieged by a feeling too inchoate to be called love but too all-pervasive to be called mere interest. As overwhelmed as I was by Prospero's attentions, still my interest in what he showed me would wander if you were too far away. I wanted to be with you, and only when you were nearby could I give myself over completely to his lessons.

At first I thought his name was 'Father', since that was what you called him, but when in my earliest attempts I called him that, he laughed – neither kindly or angrily – and corrected me, laying his hand on his own chest. *Prospero*, he said. Later, when I had grown man-sized and strong, it would be 'Master'.

Those were splendid days, that first year. Although I did not know the word, and just barely understood the principle, I felt myself part of a family. I missed my mother, and I was still often frightened to be among creatures so similar and yet so different from myself, but I also felt connected to something I had been missing all my life. My mother had been too close to me, too much a part of me – and I far too much a part of her – to give me real companionship, though the loss of her was horrible.

And compared to you and your father, she did nothing; her every day was a duplicate of the one before. But between Prospero's odd interests and your far more joyful explorations, Miranda, every day now promised something new.

One evening I fell asleep beside the hut. You and I had spent a long afternoon pulling crabs up onto the high part of the beach, then watching them hurry back to the rocks at the water's edge which contained their comfortable tidepools. We had even chosen favourites; we raced them against each other, laughing and stumbling along beside them as they bustled sideways towards safety. When we came back to the camp, Prospero had lit the fire, and he gave me a great piece of roasted coney to eat. Weary, happy, overmatched by the day's wonders, I drowsed beside you.

When I woke it was morning. A moment of animal terror at my vulnerability quickly dissipated. No one had harmed me, or seemed to intend doing so. Prospero was out walking in the forest, gathering mushrooms. You were splashing in the surf, and when you saw I was awake, you called to me, laughing. My new name in your mouth, and me reflected in your eyes. Happiness as bright and seamless as the bowl of sky overhead.

Later that day, almost vibrating with the thrill of acceptance and the relief at finally letting the better part of a year's watchfulness go slack, I climbed the hills to the thorn-hedge and my secret valley. For the two years from my orphaning until Prospero's boat ran onto the beach, the tree and the strange feelings it gave me had been the closest thing to companionship I had known. Now, elated, I wished to share my excitement. Also, in some way I wished to tell the tree that I had allies now — my feelings about the ancient pine had always had something of rivalry and distrust in them, and I had never been able to ignore its aura of power.

So that day I hurried down the thin track I had worn alongside the stream. The valley was empty but for me and a single long-eared red squirrel that clung high in the pine's branches; I could see its bright eye catch a moment's spark of sunlight. I stood within the compass of the tree-roots and shouted: *Prospero! Miranda!* Then, with an almost dizzying pride, I laid my hand on my own chest and cried: *Caliban!*

The magic of the tree seemed curiously muted that day, as though it only listened to my newfound words and pondered. I did not care. I existed. I had a name! And now I had a family.

Prospero. Prosper. If your name was an accurate summation, Miranda, his was not — although at first it seemed to be so. Yes, in those first years it seemed that he had come to raise me up, to give me the happiness that my mother could not.

What was his game? Even now I do not know. His

shadow has chilled me for more years than I can stand to think — but what was he? What did he intend for me?

Certainly when he first came to the island he can have had only the dimmest thoughts of escape and revenge. He was a powerful man, but the most of his strength was book-learning, or he would never have been overcome by his brother. His conjurings were the tricks and sleights of a hedge-wizard, spells fit mostly to amuse children or earn a few yokel-coppers at a market. Without my unwitting help, he would never have discovered the power which allowed him to regain his throne.

So what did he think to make of me? Or did he think at all of what was to come? For a man of great patience and knowledge, he often did things that made little sense. As the cloud of my ignorance evaporated somewhat over the years, and I came to see more clearly his occasional pettiness and sullen moods, I realised that he was nearly as much a creature of whim as either of his two younger charges. Could the entire matter of my upbringing, of his teaching me and moulding me and raising me beside his daughter, could it have been only the product of a momentary caprice?

That is too chilling to bear. Rather I would think of myself as the victim of a long-nursed plot. Better an enemy than an accident.

I would watch him for hours, Miranda, as he sat before the fire, making the flames form tiny shapes with a gesture of his fingers. But even as I stared at him, he stared into the blaze, his eyes remote, his thoughts roving in places I could not even begin to understand. The firelight made his sharp-hewn features almost inhuman, but in such a way that awe was combined with fierce loyalty inside me. When at last he would look up and catch me staring, he would sometimes show me just the trace of a smile. At such moments I wanted to crawl across the sand and lie down at his feet. That I had been singled out by this dark angel of subtlety made me feel more real than I had since my mother's ghastly death. Surely there must be something fine in me, I thought, that such a fiercely clever being takes pains over my existence.

In much the same way, I imagine, do your people convince themselves that they are more than scurrying two-legged insects. *Look at this world*, they tell themselves, *look at its beauty and complexity. Surely a God who could create such a thing, and has created me to see it, must love me very much.*

I hope their Creator proves more generous than my Prospero, for his gifts only seemed like kindnesses.

As the seasons turned across our island, I strove to prove myself worthy of your father's pains. I seized the bits of learning he directed my way as greedily as I had taken the fish. I spent hours reciting the names of the objects around me, never realising that although it seemed a new world was opening to me, it was only because with those names, with all those words, my own world was growing ever more distant. At the time I did not mourn the loss — its innocence, when set beside the alluring splendours of civilisation, seemed dull. But now I mourn it greatly. And the only true gift that your father's tongue has given me is that I can speak my world's elegy to someone else. So who do I ask to share my loss? You! You, who aided in its destruction. Was there ever a creature more hopelessly ensnared than I?

Still, at first it seemed that I was not losing at all, but receiving gifts hand over fist. Even my beautiful wordless world seemed gained anew, because I could take you by the hand, little Miranda, and show it to you.

We climbed the palm trees behind the sand, so high that we could look down on the birds gliding through the air along the water's edge. I showed you how to crack open the palm nuts and drink their juice; we chortled as it ran stickily down our chins, then we threw the shells as far as we could, making the gulls swerve and cry out in protest.

Hand in hand, we waded in the shallows, poking the strange sea-plants to see them shrink in what looked like fear. I lifted up a starfish whose legs were as thin as worms and laid it in your palm; when your eyes widened, my heart seemed to widen also, swelling inside my chest.

I taught you the lore of my island, although at first

I was a silent instructor. I showed you how to make a shelter from tall beach grass, and where to dig for turtle eggs when the season was right. I took you into the shadowy forest and summoned the monkeys with a hooting call: they arrived in bustling confusion, like a band of travelling players, and scolded us, then threw down twigs and leaves before hurrying away again. I pointed out the rocks where the snakes sunned themselves, and pinched your brown arm to show you what those serpents would do if you went too close. I took you to the high places and showed you where sweet water rose from the earth, a magic as fine as any of your father's sorceries.

Once, as we sat eating pomegranates in the boughs of a tree, I found myself staring at the smear of red on your mouth. I was suddenly frightened, although I did not know why. When I spat on my hand and tried to rub away the stain, you laughed and pushed at my hand until I gave up.

But even in the first blush of my enthusiasm, I did not take you to where the sow was buried. The shadow had grown a little less dark in my memory, but it was still not a place I was proud of. Nor did I show you the valley. Not then. That was a different sort of unwillingness: I was waiting for the right time. In a way I felt it was my only possession and hence my greatest gift. I wanted to save it until I knew the correct moment had come.

I sometimes slipped away to the thorn-walled valley to practise my halting speech before the silent

pine. The red squirrel was often there, and I conceived that the squirrel too should have a name. I would not, could not take your father there – as with my mother, I needed some secret I could keep from him as my own – but there were often squirrels in the trees near our camp, so one day I pulled at Prospero's sleeve and pointed to one that was digging in the earth close by.

What? That . . . what?

He smiled sourly. More than once the squirrels had come down when his back was turned and spoiled some careful arrangement of his.

Plague and pestilence, he said. *Call that 'Pest'.*

I was not yet capable of understanding a joke, of course, so 'Pest' was how I addressed the squirrel in the ancient pine from then on. I would prattle at it – and, more importantly, the tree – for hours. I knew only a few words, but I was learning more almost daily, and I burned to share my triumph with someone. You spoke nearly as well as your father. My mother was dead. So the tree was my auditor, and, in a way, my confessor. The valley was still mine and mine alone, although I was beginning to sense, if not understand, that nothing else on the island belonged to me any more. But I was radiant with my own importance and did not trouble myself. One secret place was enough.

Towards the end of my first year in Prospero's camp, wasps began to build a nest in the old tree's branches.

I suppose my mother must have taught me to swim, but I do not remember a time when I could not. Your father would have cited this as further evidence of my animal state, since the beasts of the field need no instruction in water but humans do. In any case, you did not know how to swim, so I took it upon myself to teach you. Your father, seeing the wisdom of it in a place entirely surrounded by ocean, did not interfere.

I took you to a lagoon that lay sunward along the beach some half a thousand paces from our camp. Prospero accompanied us — whether out of distrust of me or of some more menacing island inhabitant, I do not know — but remained at a distance as we splashed out through the shallows until the water nearly reached our navels. Your father seemed to be examining the trees that ringed the lagoon; at one point I saw him strip a long piece of bark from one and smell the wound in the trunk. I could not lose track of him any more than I could forget you, but it was a different sort of mark he made on my awareness: he was an upright finger of black at the edge of my eye, as though someone pointed at me in warning.

Your head in water, I said, and demonstrated by ducking myself. As I came up with my black hair blurring my eyes, you looked doubtful.

But it's all salty.

I pointed to my tightly closed mouth and thrust

my head beneath the surface once more. I kept my jaws clenched, but opened my eyes for a moment to see fronds of seaweed coiling about your legs, which shimmered grey-green in the crooked underwater light.

Now you, I said when I came up.

You shook your head and chewed your lower lip.

As the afternoon wore on your hesitation gave way and you began to enjoy yourself. From merely ducking your head you moved on to kneeling underwater for long moments, cheeks puffed out with fast-held breath; before too much longer you were gliding along below the surface, impelled by a single push off the sandy bottom. I watched you slip by, hair streaming, and reached out to feel your flank run against my hand.

Stop! you said, laughing and coughing as you came up. *That tickles!*

And all the while your father moved slowly along the rim of the lagoon, a dark shape like the shadow on a sundial.

As you were treading water in a slightly deeper spot, you stepped on something. It might have been an eel, or perhaps only a thick bulb of kelp, but you cried out in surprise and fear. I swam forward and caught you up – the difference in our sizes had become greater, and the water made you seem even lighter still, so that carrying you was like carrying air. We retreated to the shallows and I held you cradled above the water for a long moment. As I felt your weight against my arms I suddenly realised why the scarlet juice of the pomegranate had frightened me. You were real, a creature of meat and warm blood, and thus you were vulnerable. Brave Miranda was not immune to viper-stings or fish-bones. You could die, just as my mother had. You could leave me.

The moment that I held you stretched, both of us drizzling water, your shift soaking, your flesh cool against mine. I looked up to the beach. Your father had not run forward at your startled cry, or had stopped after a few steps, but he was staring intently. His eyes fixed on mine and I felt the wind growing chill on my wet skin. I set you down.

I'm tired now, and I'm hungry, you told me. *Let's go and find something to eat.*

I nodded and followed you as you splashed through the shallows towards the sand. Only when I lay curled for sleep did I realise that in the moment of your fear you had called, not '*Father*!' but '*Caliban*!'

Secrets SPIED

SOON AFTER I taught you to swim, Prospero presented me with a gift. As with the words he taught me, it was something that both gave and took away.

He had made for me a pair of breeches.

I was delighted. I had marked the differences between my betters and myself, and although I could not yet articulate my desires, I yearned to close the gap. Clothing was one of the things I coveted – or at least the idea of it fascinated me: on the few occasions I had shyly draped myself in Prospero's discarded robe or shirt I had actually felt quite itchy and entangled. And when he had seen me clad in imitation of a human being, your father had laughed and taken back my stolen finery.

But now he had changed his mind. I was burning inside with the honour of it. I had been elevated! I pulled on my new breeches, not without a first attempt that went back-to-front, then did a triumphant dance of joy. You giggled and clapped your hands to see me, so I leaped even more energetically. Even Prospero unsheathed a full smile at my capers.

And I have another thing for you, he said. *Here, little savage.*

He reached into his cloak and produced an axe, passing it to me handle-first.

The blade had been in the bottom of the boat when you and your father floated out across the ocean. Old, pitted, spattered with rust it had been, but now it gleamed. He had scraped it clean and sharpened it on a rock, then fitted it into an ironwood handle and bound it with cord.

What? I asked. *For . . . what?*

So that you may cut wood for the fire, or skin and clean a carcass, or even protect yourself against monsters, little savage. And his smile returned, thin and bright as a sliver of moon.

I looked down at my new breeches, then gazed at the beautiful, heavy thing lying in my hands. I was overwhelmed. For a moment, as tears welled in my eyes, I could see only a black and grey smear where your father sat.

Thank you, I mumbled. *Prospero, thank you.*

He waved his hand as though embarrassed. *Just be careful how you use it or I will take it back again.*

Not more than a fortnight later, Prospero took me for a walk in the forest. You came along as well, but it was my company, my advice that he wanted. He told me so. The trees seemed to part before me as I strode along.

We must build a new house, your father said. *Inland from the beach. A house where Miranda will be safe from storms and animals.*

I frowned in surprise. The only animals on the island big enough to do harm never came out of the deep forest. Still, here was a man who stood as far above me as I stood above baby turtles fumbling their way across the sand. I would not have dared to dispute with your father then.

You know the island better than I, he said. *I leave it to you to pick the spot where it should be. I ask only that we make it in a high place where I can see the ocean.*

I was delighted by this additional gift of responsibility, and as we walked up into the foothills I was pondering so hard that my head began to hurt. The clouds hung low that day, and all the island was damp and quiet, but my thoughts were loud. Where would be the best place? And what if my suggestion proved a poor one? Your father might never gift me with an important task again.

My mind was so buffeted by ideas received and then rejected that I paid little attention to where I was leading the two of you. Prospero had continued talking, speculating on the sort of house that could be built, which direction it should face to gather the light properly, and other such matters, but I was wrapped in my eager, worried considerations, and thus I did not realise my error. Without conscious thought, I led the two of you up the old deer track I had walked so many times to the perimeter of the thorn hedge that guarded my secret valley. So oblivious was I that I did not realise where we were until your father fell silent and paused, his head raised as though he heard a distant sound.

Looking around, I was struck by a sudden chill. Not this place! My only secret, my only possession! But another voice spoke in me too, a quiet voice that said: *of course, of course, this is the perfect spot.*

What is this place? Prospero asked. *It has a strange air to it.*

Nothing, I said hurriedly. *Nothing is here. Come, we go to good place.*

Your father hesitated, as though something spoke in his head as it spoke in mine. Frightened now for some reason I could not name, I plucked at his sleeve.

Not good, this place. Come along. We find good, good place for house.

He was puzzled by my agitation, but after a moment he shrugged his shoulders and allowed me to lead him away.

Grateful, relieved as though I had avoided some dire fate, I brought you hurriedly back down the hillside — skirting widely the place where I had buried the sow — and up into another clump of hills.

Better here, I said – and as it turned out, I had unwittingly chosen a likely spot, although my concern had been only to bring you both away from the thorns and the hidden valley. *Look*, I said, pointing. *You see ocean there. And water comes from the ground here.*

It was indeed a good choice, and Prospero, despite a few lingering, considering looks at me, quickly agreed. A natural fold in the south face of the hill would keep the worst of the winds at bay, and a spring of clear water seeped from the ground not a hundred paces down the hillside. In the deepest cleft of the fold stood a large old fig tree whose spreading branches would provide not just fruit, but also shelter from sun and rain.

Prospero smoothed his beard with long fingers as he surveyed the site. You had already run down the hill towards the water, and were on your knees splashing water into your mouth.

It's good, Father! you shouted.

I think you are right, little savage, he said. *We will build here.*

The moment of fear beside the thorn hedge still haunted me, so I did not dance again, but I was very happy.

If I had only known, Miranda. If I could have read and understood your father's grammaries, perhaps I might have discovered in one of them a spell to stop time . . . for those days, those few months, perhaps two short years in all, were the happiest I would have. How I long for a window I could open into my own past so I could call a warning to my younger self. *Stop there*, I would shout. *Go no farther!*

But as I think on it, perhaps I should open an earlier window: by the day we found your new home, Prospero had already sown in me the seeds of corruption, though I did not yet understand what would hatch out. Thus, it might be better to find that young No-Name crouching on the rock and give him some warning instead. I could tell him to run away . . . or even to take stones and kill you both the first night you slept upon my island. If he had buried you both in a shameful hole beside the she-pig, I cannot believe that his punishment in some afterlife could be more dreadful than the ruin of my life now.

But I had not a glimpse of this, of any of this. I was a little manikin, dressed in human clothing but by no means a human, made to dance for the entertainment of a secretive old man and his spoiled child. I was a puppet, useful only so long as I amused.

Or worked, for that was where your father's thoughts were leading. I believe he had seen the size of me in my young bones, and intended to get full measure from my strength. Like a mule that is whipped up and down the streets all day, then is grateful for a handful of oats when evening falls, I was to be encouraged towards usefulness by small favours. A cruel, scheming man, your father.

But, strangely, even now I hope that he did not

entirely understand what he did to me . . . for a part of me loves him. There is a joke for you! A part of me loves him still, that terrible stone on which my life ran and foundered. The awe, the amazement, the joy at the simplest attention from Prospero has not entirely faded. If I had found him alive in Milan, I would have wept before I killed him, and not just from rage. Just as I will weep before this night is out, Miranda.

I was set to work. Oh, he was not so foolish as to call it such, and indeed he laboured at my side at first, teaching me such arts as were needed for the building of fences, of walls. To me it seemed like more magic — at that time your world was all so foreign and strange I could see little difference between the sorcery of words, the witchcraft of dancing puppets, and the wizardry of ridgepole, cruck, and thatched roof.

I worked eagerly, anxious to show that the manhood-gifts he had given me were not wasted. From sunrise until the sky was purple with approaching night I hacked away at fallen trees, splitting them and then splitting again, cutting the pieces to length with the knotted vine-rope your father gave me for measuring. Huge bundles bent my back as I carried them up the hillside, but I gave not a word of complaint.

Even the idea of the house was fabulous to me. When I first saw him draw it in the dirt, saw the interior walls that would divide it into different sections like the chambers of a nautilus, I was astonished. What else could I think but that Prospero had himself invented the idea of a house with more than one room? It confirmed his other-worldly genius.

We built the fence first. I wonder now what exactly it was that led your father to seal off the ground before digging even the first post-hole of the house. Some dim, troubling memory of his suborned guards coming for him in the middle of the night? Or some less specific fear, the kind that creeps on a man when he is alone in a wild place? In any case, we built that fence strong and high, with the tops of the posts sharpened like my old fish-spear.

Next we built the house itself, a great rectangle of timbers constructed around a stone fireplace and chimney — one wonder piled on another! As the weeks went by and Prospero saw that I had learned my carpentry lessons well, he spent less time watching over me and returned once more to his wandering ways. Often he took you with him, continuing the lessons in speech, history, and natural philosophy which for a while I had shared . . . until he found this new and apparently more important task for me.

The sense of being in a family was not altogether gone. On some days your father would sit nearby, chipping with a stone adze at some delicate but important item, a gate-hinge perhaps, or weaving a window-screen from the fronds of the tall beach palms. At those times you would help me, holding a post straight while I laboured to fill the hole around it with clay, or steadying a board that I was struggling to cut evenly. Sometimes, against my mild protests – not for a moment did I want to appear a shirker! – you would even carry some of the lashed bundles of wood up from where I had cut them. You were growing too, Miranda. I could not help seeing how your legs were lengthening; I could not be entirely unmoved by the curve of muscle beneath your soft brown skin. Prospero seldom spoke, but as his hands flew gracefully through the motions of his task like nest-building birds, his eyes watched us always.

A full year I laboured on the house, positioning each beam, wedging each joint with my own hands. And as I pridefully watched Prospero's sand-sketch growing into reality on the hillside, I felt myself growing, too – growing and becoming. Becoming a man, I thought. Becoming a son, I sometimes dared to hope.

The night we laid the last of the roof-thatch, we had a celebration. Twelve moons had waxed and waned, and the thirteenth was already half-eaten, since the day I had led you and your father away from the valley. Now the house was finished. I did not understand then how much larger than necessity we had built it, nor how much faster the work would have gone had Prospero continued to assist me. I knew only that I had done something that made me proud, and that your father was pleased with it.

As if to atone for his dereliction – a dereliction of which I was not then aware – your father had trapped and killed a pig. I thought it must be one of the piglets of the murdered sow, and when he dragged it back to the house I was swept by a moment of superstitious panic, but I was reassured by the sturdy walls we had raised and by your father's unusual good humour. I helped him dig a pit, then we shovelled in the coals from the fire, wrapped the carcass in plantain leaves, and covered it over.

Come here, Caliban, he said then. *You too, Miranda.*

He so seldom used my name that my fear came back to me. Had he somehow discovered what had happened to the mother of the animal now smoking in the pit? Was I to be punished for the crime I had committed, the crime that, though not understood, had long plagued my memory?

Instead he produced a bottle, corked and capped with lead. It was something I had not seen before, though I had eagerly nosed through all his civilised possessions whenever I had found the opportunity.

It is from Portugal, he said. *I have kept it aside for just such a happenstance. For tonight we celebrate a new home.*

With equal deftness, Prospero conjured bowls. He

poured just a splash into yours, but filled mine and his sloshing to the brim.

Drink, little savage. We have built a true house where such a thing never existed.

I was pleased and honoured, but I also felt a small tug of unease. Was not the place my mother and I had lived a house? Was it too humble to be considered a human place? And was I still mostly animal because I would never have thought to build a magnificent home without Prospero's urging?

Nevertheless, I lifted the bowl and let the blood-coloured liquid run down my throat. Then I coughed it out again, so explosively I feared my liver and lights would follow. It had nothing like the sweetness I expected from such a valued prize, but was harsh and sour.

Your father laughed. So did you after you saw that I was not actually dying.

Do not swill the stuff as if it were stream-water. It is precious, and you are not used to precious things. Small sips. Thusly. And he lifted his own bowl to his mouth. You drank some too, Miranda, then gave Prospero a puzzled look.

It's just wine, Father, you protested. Ah, how my heart plummeted that you should dismiss something so frighteningly heady! You had drunk wine since you were a small child.

But it's older and better and more so, was his answer. *And we shall not water it. Not tonight!*

And indeed we drank much, although it was some time before I could swallow it down my ragged throat without wincing. I had no idea why real people should drink such stuff, but I would not be shamed by you; also, it was a gift from your father to me, a rare thing, a thing to be savoured.

I have told you that my mother would sing some-times, wordless croons that I could neither under-stand nor ignore. That night, as the wine boiled in my brain, I felt snatches of her songs float through my ears as if she had returned and stood behind my shoulder. It should have been a frightening feeling, but it was not. The night was becoming oddly warm and entirely welcoming. I heard my mother's voice in the hiss of wind through the thatch and in the burble of talk between you and your father.

I drank more wine. We drained the bottle dry and ate roast pork and plantains steaming from the cooking-pit; I held the singed ears of our victim to my head and chased you across the hillside, both of us squealing and giggling. Later, dizzy from exertion, I watched the light-flecked sky revolving around the very spot where I sat, as though each star bent to look at me . . . at the little savage who had built a house, who lived with real people, who had a name!

I stood, unsteadily, and followed you and your father down the hill to the beach. Prospero carried a burning brand which bobbed along before me like a firefly. The noises of the night forest were loud, and my mother's songs hummed and murmured in my ears. We reached the water's edge and stood watching the white moon-froth slide up on the sand. I felt full of something strong, something as old as the tides and yet inextricably a part of me. I heard my mother's song, but at the same time I heard my own name, the thing I had been given that now was . . . me.

Ca-li-ban! I sang. You turned to stare at me, Miranda. Your eyes widened with surprise and amusement, but you did not smile. Your father did not smile either; he stood with his arms folded on his chest as I took a few steps out into the receding waves.

Ban! Ban! Cali-cali-ban! I raised my voice and looked up, searching for the moon that had been my companion even after my mother died, but I could not find it. I sang on, fitting the words to a melody that might have been my mother's, or might have come through some other door in my drunken head.

Ban! Ban! Caliban! Ban! Ban! Caliban!

As I sang I began to splash through the surf, whirling, scattering the foam with my hands.

Ban! Ban! Caliban!
Cali-Cali-ban!

I sang louder and louder and spun faster and faster until my brain tipped over in my head and I tumbled into the water. Laughing, you pulled me up and helped me stumble back to the beach. My head still spun, but I could no longer remember why I had begun singing.

We sat down on the sand, you and I, but your father remained at the water's edge. I huddled shivering beside you, then all of my innards abruptly rushed into my mouth and leaped out between my teeth. The fit of sickness did not last long. When I had finished, you covered the spew with sand, then returned to the water's edge and brought back sea-water in cupped hands to wash my face. Your father only watched; in the dark, I could not see his expression.

When I was a little recovered, Prospero cried: *Watch.*

He plucked up the burning torch he had planted in the sand, then waved it in the air, printing a circle of fire against the blackness. When he had finished, the ring still remained there, blazing. He made other shapes, drew pictures of animals and birds and fish, wrote what seemed words in characters unlike any I had seen in his books. He made the hanging fires change colours, first red, then dripping silver, then a blue that pulsed like a cricket's song constructed of light. We watched. You clapped your hands with joy.

After a while your father waved his spidery fingers and the flame-pictures fell to the surf in smoking gobbets. Steam hissed and rose, hiding Prospero for a moment. When it had faded, he was standing over us, a blackness in which no stars hung.

I do not remember much of the journey back up the hill. The sounds of the forest were more muted, and Prospero's torch seemed farther away than on the trip down, as though it burned at the bottom of a deep pit.

When we reached the new house, he said to me: *You have been sick. Sleep by the fire. You can wash yourself in the morning.*

I curled up next to the firepit. I felt a moment of sadness that you and he were going off to other rooms, but the coals were warm, and very soon I rolled down into sleep.

When I look back on the year or two that followed, I see the world hardening like mud beneath a strong sun. Although the world of my earlier childhood had seemed dull set against the novelty of you new-comers, I see now that it had been a fluid, ever-changing thing, with only a few verities – my mother's breathing, her dry, salty scent, the dark-daubed walls of our hut – to give it shape. Every day I had risen with the idea of what would come to me with the sun. Each night, as my mother had mumbled and snored nearby, I had wondered with lazy complacency what the next day would bring.

But after the new house was finished, the strong rays of your father's will began to solidify my once-formless days. There was water to be drawn from the stream for drinking, bathing, cooking, and most of all, for your father's strange experiments. Wood was needed, too: the fires in the front yard, the main room, and of course his working-chamber were never to be allowed to go out. The axe he had given to me those many moons ago had by this time been resharpened more times than I could tally on my calloused fingers and toes.

At first Prospero asked me to do these things as a favour, a kindness from me that would allow him more time for gathering leaves and seeds or for teaching you your catechism. But when repetition and the passage of time had made those same deeds routine instead of extraordinary, he began to criticise any small error or dereliction.

I was distracted for a while by the wonders your father produced in his new house, his castle in the wilderness. He had brought a surprising amount of things with him out of Milan – I suppose you have forelock-tugging Gonzalo to thank for that – but he had kept them well secured, doling out a glance at one of his books or a touch of some of the finer pieces of cloth only when he felt moved to reward me . . . which was infrequently. This, of course, only made me more hungry for his secrets, more dissatisfied with my own state, but without any accompanying belief that I might better myself by other means than Prospero's largess. I peered from the corners of my eyes at your father's treasures like a bird eyeing a larger bird's worm – like any outsider, I avidly watched those I envied, the better to imitate them. The truly surprising thing about that bottle of Portugal wine was not just that he

produced it at all, but that I had not even guessed at its existence.

Now, as though the stout fence around the compound made him feel safer, he retrieved many of the precious things he had kept hidden and decked the new abode with them. Books! How he could stow such a quantity in that puny boat of yours I cannot imagine, but I carried them up the hill in great armloads. Not that I saw much more of them than that, for they were immediately put away in his 'chamber', as he called it, and a great iron lock – more of the booty of Milan – was run through the door-handle. I portered countless other oddities for him as well: chests of thin crystal vessels of various sizes – what did I know of glass? – cutting and chopping tools in a dozen different styles; jars full of odd liquids, both cloudy and clear, many distilled since he had come to the island; even a human skull. He had to tell me what this last was, since I had only seen the headbones of animals. Prospero said it was the True Orphic Cranium, whatever that might mean, and made little jokes about it singing to him at night.

What else he carried up to the house in his own deep pockets I do not know, but I am as certain as I am of my breath and heartbeat that he did not entrust his most valuable items to my willing but sometimes clumsy hands. During the final months of building, when your father had abandoned the carpentry entirely to me, he had carved himself a staff – a walking-stick, as I thought it, strangely festooned in ribbons and feathers and shards of sparkling, jagged glass. He carried that himself – he would never let me even touch it – and when all was in place, he waved it back and forth in the open doorway for no little time, mumbling, his eyes open but not looking at anything. Then he locked the door behind him and did not come out of his chamber for the rest of the day.

He had given me several tasks to do, but I was happy enough to obey since for that afternoon I had your company without your father's oversight. When I had finished the hauling and carrying, I led you back down the hill to see a plover's nest I had found. We pierced the shell of an egg and drank the cold, salty contents. I told you, in my still-awkward speech, that I was pleased and lucky to be your friend.

You smiled, then filled the empty shell full of sand and let it sift back out through the hole we had made.

Prospero moved me out of the house. Or, rather, I was never fully allowed to move in. After that first night on the floor beside the fire, I was given my own small chamber – a shed, in plain words – at the house's far western side. It was no smaller than the hut in which I had been raised, so the size did not trouble me, but it was far from where your father slept, and it was farther still from you, Miranda. That gave me pain.

You do not know the ways of our folk, he told me. His blue eyes were cold as stones tumbling in the ocean depths, but his voice was utterly reasonable. *She is becoming a young lady, and needs her privacy. It is thus in our houses in Milan. And I must have my own elbow-room. I have many things to think on. The place I have given you is yours alone, and you may do with it as you wish. Bring in any fetishes or tokens that suit you. Make an altar to your mother's god Setebos if you wish. No man can say fairer.*

But, I thought – and even the sourness of the unspoken idea seemed like a form of heresy – how can you *give* me a single room in a house which I built?

Words, at first my adored new friends, were already beginning to show another face.

But I said nothing out loud; if Setebos meant nothing to me – and may have meant as little to my mother, for all I know – I was content to fill my room with my own collections of colourful stones and the abandoned skins of snakes. Only occasionally was I troubled by the gnawing thought that not long ago I had been lord of an island entire, but now my holdings were reduced to a single cell at the outskirts of Prospero's house.

A single cell . . . and a hidden valley. For I still went to that place from time to time, and it had remained a secret, even from your father's rapacious curiosity. Would that it had stayed that way!

*

The wasps had completed their labours; the nest, a grey thing that seemed made from parchment, hung in the branches of the old pine like a single tear depending from an eyelash. It was low enough that I could sit against the tree's trunk and watch the wasps moving in and out, crawling to and fro across its surface as though it were the entire world.

As they crawled, they hummed, a sound sometimes lulling, other times redolent of menace. But since they did not fly at me or otherwise offer me harm, I learned to ignore them, although once I had the strange feeling I could hear a voice in the general murmur, as I had heard my mother's song in the night-sounds when I had drunk too much.

And as the wasps droned, I talked – speaking to the air, or perhaps the pine, or my dead mother. I searched for words to describe my yearnings, I mourned the things that I had lost; sometimes I even spoke to you, Miranda, and tested the sound of things I longed to tell you but did not dare. I was in love, you see, but it was only intermittently a happy thing. For all the joy that your proximity brought me, it also made me feel crude and dull. Too many times I had tried to do something brave or clever and had instead made myself foolish. So, on those days I sat beneath the ancient tree, as frequently as I spoke words that I wished to say to you, or even that I dreamed you might someday say to me, I also chided myself as thoroughly as Prospero ever had. I took my own song of the celebration night and hung on it a mocking tail.

> *Ban! Ban! Caliban!*
> *Likes to think that he's a man!*

I sang and babbled to the sky. The pine tree nodded above my head as the wind whispered and hissed through the branches. The busy wasps mumbled in their grey parchment house.

Ha! I see you look towards the bedchamber door, Miranda! I hear what you hear, but must tell you it is only the settling of beams, not the footfalls of a rescuer. In any case, here is my hand, not a moment's distance from your white throat. I have planned my course well: we have time enough for me to do all that I need. Time enough. I am coming to the nub of your black, black treachery, so I do not doubt you wish for someone to interrupt, even at the cost of your life. Now, listen!

It was one of those days when your father was bent on some exacting piece of work and the house was full of stinks. From time to time he would burst forth from his chamber accompanied by a swirl of foul-smelling smoke, ordering me to fetch this or that – a heavy stone, a dipper full of water. Through the murk I could see the scarlet eyes of small fires burning on the table inside.

The third or fourth time he erupted through the door he demanded that I go and pick for him a bunch of leaves from a particular yellow-flowered tree, of which there were few on the island.

I should send Miranda, who has a defter hand, he grumbled, *but she has wandered off. Ruination on the girl, who will not help her father, the author of her life and freedom! Go, my savage, and fetch me the leaves.*

Waving his arms so that his sleeves billowed as wildly as the smoke, he plunged back into his chamber, tugging the door shut behind him. Whatever his labours, they did not seem to be going well; in the preceding weeks he had shown an increasingly foul temper.

Hurry! he cried from inside. *The mixture is almost ready, and I still must fire the kiln!*

Growling under my breath, for I grew less and less fond of acting his bond-servant, I went out.

It was high afternoon and the day was hot. As might be guessed with an errand so apparently needful of haste, the leaves proved elusive: I went up and down through the flowering groves along the hillside surrounding the house, but found none of the yellow-blossomed trees. I was all a-sweat before an hour had passed, and tired withal, but I felt sure it was better not to go back at all than to return empty-handed. So I hunted farther down the hillside, pushing my way through the thick undergrowth. I found one of the streams that flowed from the highlands and stopped to bathe my face and drink some of the sweet water, then I followed the course of the stream-bed down. I had a dim memory that where the water rolled off a cliff-face and into a pool, there had once been a tiny copse of the trees whose leaves Prospero wanted. It was a longer walk than I had hoped for, but I had exhausted all the possible spots nearby.

Birds were shouting raucously to each other in the canopy above my head, and the watercourse was only a little quieter. The damp air and the mist on my face made me even more aware of how much I had come to dislike the hot fumes in Prospero's house. Perhaps, I thought, when I had found the leaves and delivered them I would invent an errand to come back here so that I might be alone for a while, relishing the solitude.

Then, as I felt the ground slope down sharply beneath my feet, foretokening the waterfall, I heard singing. I stopped for a moment and listened, and although I knew the voice as well as I knew my own, I was covered all over in chills at the sweetness of it.

So then, I told myself after a little while—*Miranda too had a yearning to escape her father, and has picked the very spot which has lured me. I will surprise her, then we will laugh at the way we have played truant.*

I moved along the lip of stone where the stream splashed over, listening all the while to your happy song. When I had gone some four or five dozen paces from the top of the cataract, I could at last look down to the pool where the falling water churned. There at the water's edge was a stand of the golden-flowered trees, each with its complement of spiky, dark-green leaves. But the trees, though the object of my quest, were suddenly as nothing to me.

I stood and stared, helpless, my tongue stuck to the roof of my mouth, the joking shout I was about to loose frozen in my throat. You stood knee-deep in the pool beneath the waterfall, Miranda, naked and beautiful and as splendid as Heaven itself.

I see you flinch, see your lips curl to spit some epithet at me, but you do me an injustice. I was not spying, had no dream of anything but surprising my friend. And as for the thoughts that suddenly whirled in my head – the thoughts that now bring a blush to your cheek, a reddening I can see even by candlelight! – they were the thoughts of an innocent. As was my heart an innocent's heart.

Can you doubt it? Can there have been any thinking creature on the earth more untouched by base lechery than I? In my years of life, I had never seen a flesh-and-blood woman unclothed. The only other female of my experience had been my gnarled stick of a mother, and even she never undressed before me. In fact, I much doubt she ever disrobed from the moment she first set her foot upon the island.

And there you stood, clad in the raiment that your

God gave you at birth – no, I tell a lie, for you were fast becoming a woman. In any case, there you stood, made as Nature wished you made. And Nature wrought wonderfully well when she created you, Miranda. Your nakedness was like a candle in a twilit room. May all the spirits of my island strike me dead if I lie: I could not have looked away had my life been at stake. You were so beautiful that it hurt me.

You stood in the streaming, shimmering curtain of the waterfall with your back to me. Your tangled hair was piled high upon your head and held by your fingers, your face tilted up to the cataract. You had stopped singing to drink. Such perfect, unthinking freedom I saw there, such joy in the feel of cold water splashing over you! It is an image that will haunt me to my last breath. Whoever stands over my dying body will see it reflected in my eyes.

I had seen goddesses and famous beauties in your father's books, and had felt a strong, attracted attention in myself as I stared at them – so much that I had taken to stealing glances at those particular woodcuts only when I was alone, not understanding my shame or fascination, but feeling them strongly all the same. But as a few etched lines representing a cloud on a parchment page are to the roiling, ever-changing magnificence of the true sky, so were the dim figures that had so captured my interest when placed against the reality of you, Miranda.

Every line of you, from your long back and gently rounded rump to your legs as muscular and graceful as a young deer's, the soft geometry of your spine and shoulder-blades moving beneath the skin, every inch of you covered in sparkling water like an armour of pure sunlight . . . the sight washed over me and changed me forever. My breathing sped, sounding loud and harsh in my own ears even above the steady rush of the water. I wanted you, wanted you more than anything I had ever desired, although I could not imagine what form the having might take. So powerful was that desire, though, that for a moment in my confusion I became the cannibal of your father's prejudice: I wanted to possess you and your beauty so fiercely that I could almost imagine devouring you.

At that moment, as if the confused thoughts flitting in my head took visible form, a bright shape appeared from the place behind the cataract, flew rapidly back and forth for a moment, then sped across the clearing. It was a bright blue bird, identical in my eye to that which had watched me from the old pine on the day I had discovered the valley. Its movements or the garishness of its colour caught your attention. You lowered your hands, letting your hair snake down onto your shoulders, and turned to watch its flight.

Startled, I flung myself down against the edge of the precipice, terrified you would see me. Why I should feel such an interloper when only a few years before we had splashed innocently together through the ocean shallows in nakedness and near-nakedness, I could not say, but something about my hunger told me that this was different. I lay flat, but still kept my eyes raised above the cornice of rock.

More wonders! Your breasts were rounded, soft as ripe fruit, the tips pushing out boldly like the noses of young rabbits. And beneath your beautiful golden belly you were tufted with the same brown hair that dusted the hollows under your arms . . . but there was nothing else where your legs joined, a lack that was to me both pitiful and a little frightening. For a long moment I wondered if the great difference in our making were some further indication of the difference between my kind and yours.

As if to remind me of that disparity, I felt my own flesh stiffen where I lay pressed against the ground. The hunger came again, but it was not a hunger of the belly; rather it stretched to all parts of me, as strong in my eyes and twitching fingertips as anywhere else, but strongest of all in the warm heaviness of my groin where I rubbed against the cloth of my breeches.

There I lay as you finished your bathing, helpless, desperate, consumed by incomprehensible passion, my thoughts struggling as confoundedly as blindfolded armies. At last you dressed and went away, but still I lay on my belly like one struck down by lightning.

*

I returned to the house as the sun was setting. So brain-baffled was I that I had neglected to harvest Prospero's leaves. He flew into a fury and shouted at me, called me a foolish, ungrateful animal and other things, bellowed that I had spoiled his entire day's work, that I was not worth an instant of the time he had lavished on my education. I took it all with bowed head, although a part of me smouldered into anger that I should have to endure such abuse from him. You, perhaps ashamed that he should call me those names, or perhaps merely wishing to escape the noise, retired to your own chamber.

For my crimes I was sent to sleep out of doors that night, and was given no food, but these punishments meant less than nothing to me, so caught up was I in agonies far more complicated, far more deep-reaching.

A Shattered TREE

IN THE SUBSTANTIAL part of the year that followed
my surprising you at your bath, the character of all
our relationships continued to change – for the
worse, from my outlook.

Less and less did Prospero even pretend to treat
me as a man, much less as family. Although there
were still flashes of his old kindness, I saw his anger
far more often, but for the most part received only
cold indifference. As long as I did what he bade me
do, I was allowed to sleep in my small room at the
edge of the house and share what communal meals
there were. Still, even when I was part of the
company, his conversation was almost all directed
at you, his daughter.

I understand that among your folk those who
serve you are considered to be scarcely more
important than a table or chair, that secrets are
spoken before them with no concern since they are
not seen as true people. I have felt this chilling

treatment, and I know it to be something that eats away the soul. Even you began, if unconsciously, to ape your father's treatment of me. Once you told me to go and fetch your sewing. Told me, not asked! I did as you wished, but afterward I stood in the trees beyond the house, well out of earshot, and sobbed until I thought I would be sick.

But you did not realise what you did, and still in the main treated me like a friend, which was a balm that soothed most hurts your father gave me. Yet your mere proximity brought on certain other ills of the spirit that nothing could heal. The innocence with which I had first loved you was gone, although I was paradoxically still too innocent to put a name to what had changed it. I dreamed of you as I had seen you bathing in the pool, or savoured memories of other glances I had stolen at you in unguarded moments, for my eye was as greedy for you now as was my heart.

We walked together sometimes, and spoke often, although my duties and your education and your own chores – increasingly, the construction and mending of your apparel – kept us apart most days. You now went as fully and even richly dressed as if you were living in the luxurious court of Milan. That your father should have, in his moment of exile, bargained for fine cloth with his half-conspirator, Gonzalo, only teaches me the bizarre priorities of civilised men. In any case, you took on as a suitable task the making of outfits for yourself and the repair of your father's. But they were clothes inspired by the illustrations in your father's library, fantastical and pointless to my untrained eye. Even when you walked in the deep forest, you now wore clothing more appropriate to life in a servant-staffed house. As Prospero had recreated such a house as best he could – despite having only one rather reluctant servitor – so you seemed to be trying to push the rusticity of the island away and replace it with some laughably false civility.

But although I saw this with surprising clarity, I could not bring myself to scorn you. For one thing, I knew you did it mostly to please your father, although the prettiness of the fabric delighted you and you found the constructive labour soothing. But for me it was the knowledge of what lay beneath your garments that made your clothed form a torture to me in a way it had not been before. Every sight of you now reminded me of your natural, unhidden state: the sway of your hips or curve of your haunch, even beneath heavy fabric, shortened my breath. The line of your long neck, the gentle swell of honey-hued breasts above your bodice, seemed an invitation most urgent – but to what or to where I could not quite understand.

Also, and impossibly, I wished that somehow you could find in me the same fascination I took in you – I even fumblingly attempted to pray, for in this as in other things I imitated my betters. I looked nothing like your father, but neither did you, nor did I look like my mother, save that in the darkness of my complexion I mimicked her as your pale skin did your sire's. I had grown much in the five years since the advent of you and your father and had by now reached my adult height, although I was a little smaller in the trunk and arms than I am now — bearing the burden of desertion has strengthened and broadened me, perhaps. I did not know if I was fair or foul, but could only hope that you found me good to look upon. I had no idea of what beauty was, except insomuch as I knew that I would rather look at you than at anything else beneath the sky or of it.

My preoccupation with you was driving me to the brink of madness. I swallowed every insult your father gave me, even shrugged off the occasional proddings or smacks from his walking-stick, all because being near you, even in pain, was infinitely superior to being anywhere else.

There came a day that was like many others, but for one thing: Prospero was sick. Whether from the inhalations of the noxious fumes of his work or from some other contagion, I do not know. The work that had seemed his greatest joy now gave him only grief — in fact, I believe that he had finally realised he could not discover the magical means to effect revenge against the usurpers or even to escape his banishment — so perhaps it was despair that sickened him. Whatever the truth, your father climbed back into his bed, complaining bitterly of his aches and fluxions, and kept us busy all the morning bringing him this or that apothecarial substance from his table, or building or banking the fire, until at last a little before noon he fell into a deep sleep.

Hear me! I raise this as evidence before you, Miranda: whatever crimes you may claim against me, it was not I who invited you outside the house. And if your love for your father was as complete as you would claim, why did you not sit patiently by his sickbed like a doting child? The answer, I guess, is that you were nearly as tired of his tyrannies as I was, and for far less reason. You had seen that his illness did not seem anything like mortal, for all his complaints, and were anxious to have an interlude of freedom in the clean air.

How little fortitude you possessed, who had not tasted a fraction of the suffering I had! A single afternoon of his ill-tempered orders was enough to drive you away.

Walk with me, Caliban, you said. *I desire some air and sunshine, but I am afraid there might be serpents.*

You, who once ran bare-legged through the grass! Could you not simply say you wished my company? Or were you truly worried? Had you really become such a different thing, a mock-lady, queening it in the fastness of a wild island?

But these are my thoughts now. At that moment, in that place, all I could do was tremble with pleasure that your thought was the same as my own. You wished to be away from your father, and you wished me at your side. Perhaps you were beginning to feel some of the same things I was! You would be my partner and friend again, and the growing loneliness would end.

As we walked down the hillside in the bright sun, I felt my side touch yours. Oh, when one is in love, Miranda, what a wealth of feeling springs from such slight things! For a moment it seemed to validate my most secret hopes, reassure me of our unspoken closeness.

The bottom of the hill was swaddled in trees, and for a little while we moved through green darkness and light as spotty as summer rain. As I watched the needle-thin beams move across your hair like a caress, I saw that you had grown fully as tall as I — perhaps even a little taller. But I had grown in other ways: my arms were each nearly as broad as your slim legs, and a thin pelt of dark fur had sprouted on my face and body. I had hopes — oh, Miranda, the way folly dogs us! — of growing a beard as long and impressive as your father's. He was the only man I knew; I was doomed to awkward imitation, as even now my heart's agony comes tumbling out in *his* mother tongue.

And as I stood contemplating without understanding the wonderful difference in our forms, you took my hand. By that simple act, with whatever intent you might have had, you doomed us all in a hundred, hundred doleful ways. From that moment our lives have tumbled towards this hour, this circumstance, with the implacability of a boulder nudged off its perch at the top of a mountain.

Your hand curled around mine, cool and inviting. I was stunned, since you had not touched me except in an accident of passing for a long, long while. For years I had waited like a starving beggar outside a house far greater than any I had built for your father – greater than any ever built of such crude things as wood or stone – and now you had suddenly opened the door to me. Or so it seemed. How could I ever repay you? How could I ever make known to you what your closeness, your kindness, your astonishing beauty meant? I had only one gift worthy of you.

Miranda, I said, almost unable to speak for the sudden thickness of my tongue. *I . . . I wish to show you something.*

You looked at me, but did not release my hand. Your eyes sparkled, full of pleasure at our intrigue.

What would you have me see?

But I could say no more, for fear my pounding heart would leap out of my bosom. I clutched your fingers as a hunted crab clings to the walls of its undersea lair, then I led you back up into the hills.

I stopped at last before the thorn hedge. You pulled

your hand away, panting for breath; I had hurried you mercilessly and you were more than a little cross.

What is this, Caliban? Have you dragged me halfway across the island to show me some bushes? They are not even pretty.

So saying, you extended your hand and before I could stop you, laid hold of one of the branches, then pulled back with a cry.

Merciful Lord! Something has stung me!

You held the finger up so I could see the shining bead of blood. I was ashamed and somehow terribly excited.

They are thorns, I said throatily. *Do not touch them, please, my Miranda.*

You raised an eyebrow. *This is far to have brought me so that I can be stabbed almost to the death.*

I raised a gesturing arm toward the hedge, thinking to tell you just enough to make savoury with anticipation the sight that would soon greet you, then stopped, bewildered. For how could I show you the valley? Could I ask you, in your fine dress of black and gold and sky blue, to crawl on your back through the dust – hard labour beneath an infinitude of thorns?

And yet what else could I do? I had brought you here to give you my gift. The moment seemed so delicately balanced; surely if I took you away again, unrewarded, I would sink in your estimation.

Stand here, Miranda. I hurried a short way down

the hillside, searching frantically. A kind of madness was on me.

This is a strange trick, Caliban. We should not leave Father alone too long. He may wake up and be upset that I am not there.

Already I had found what I sought, and was crouched upon the ground, rubbing, rubbing. My heart was speeding, but I was determined not to lose this chance. Just as my arms became so tired I felt I could labour no longer, a small spark dropped from the sticks into the pile of crumbled bark and dry grass.

See, Miranda, see! I said as tiny flames began to lick upward. I gathered the pile of smoking tinder and took it to the hedge, ignoring your questions in my obsessive attention to keeping the fire alight.

A longish time passed before the tough thorn bushes caught, but by now I had captured your attention. You watched almost as raptly as I while first the dry mulch beneath, then the leaves, then the horny stalks themselves began to burn. As the flames chewed away at the thorns, I laboured to keep the fire from spreading, throwing dirt on every outbreak except the growing orange road through the thorn-fence. As the area nearest the edge collapsed into glowing coals, exhausted of food for the flames, I crushed its smouldering remnants beneath a large stone.

It was hard work; several times the fire threatened to escape my control and cause a general conflagration, but I was everywhere. When you understood at last what I was doing, you helped too, throwing handfuls of earth on such outrunners of the blaze as I pointed out. Within a short while your beautiful costume was stained with soil and ashes, but you were smiling. It was a children's game, at least for you, Miranda, and the child in you was not yet gone.

At last I had burned a path through the hedge, not considering that what had been done in such haste might be regretted anon. I made sure the last of the fires were out, then led you through. The afternoon sun was now high and strong, and the stream glinted beneath its rays like a train of precious stones.

What is this place? Your voice was soft, as though you recognised that we now shared a secret.

It is for you, Miranda. I give it to you.

Already I was thoroughly infected with your father's having and keeping and giving. To name something is to begin to possess it. What a wealth of greed there is in your civilised speech!

We walked down the streambank towards the marshy meadow and the sentinel pine. I saw a flirt of russet in the treetops and knew that Pest was there. I called to him gaily, as to a friend. In the poverty of my acquaintances, I suppose he was.

As you looked around, your face aglow with wonder, I felt as though I had found my pinnacle of joy.

It is a beautiful place, you whispered.

For you, for you, for you, I said, and did a little dance.

There was another bright flash of colour in the branches of the old pine, a smear of bright blue. It was the bird that had watched me so intently that first day. On one or two other occasions it had returned, but long since had seemed to give up pride of place to the red squirrel. If the tree were a Prospero, I had imagined, then the cerulean bird was a Caliban, a servant who had lost some of his novelty but was allowed to skulk about in the background.

As we crossed the meadow you asked me questions about the valley. I told you how I had discovered it, and in my halting fashion, why I loved it. You knelt beside the stream to wash your hands, then loosened your bodice and splashed your neck and breastbone with cool water. I felt exhilarated, yet peaceful. We settled at last on the sheltered ground, against the trunk of the ancient pine tree. You surveyed the upward sweep of the hillside, the pocket jewel that was my secret place.

It is very beautiful. You took my hand again. *Thank you for bringing me here.*

The murmur of the wasp nest overhead was a sweet song in my ears. The chirping of other insects in the long grass, the trickle of the stream, even the skittering claws of Pest on the branches above, filled me with a great happiness. I was in the one place that was still mine, and you were with me. I leaned closer, putting my mouth against your ear, and was so struck by the smell of your hair that for a moment I could not speak.

It is all for you, Miranda. I . . . I love you.

There was a long moment's silence in which I heard only the blood in my temples. At last you said: *And you are my dear, dear friend, Caliban.*

It was not precisely what I wanted to hear, but it was something. The hot afternoon had still gone far beyond anything I could have hoped for. I gently trailed my fingers – roughened by servitude – down the length of your neck.

You make me shiver.

It is the touch of a loving friend, Miranda. I pressed my face against your cheek again, sucking in your scent. *I am your servant. I want only to make you happy. I . . . I want . . .*

But I did not know what I wanted.

Your breathing is so loud, Caliban . . . !

My other hand coiled about your waist and held you snug while my fingers dipped down from your neck and smeared the drops of water beading above your faintly freckled breasts. Your bodice was still untied and I loosened it further.

What are you doing? You sounded a little surprised, but I heard no fear.

I . . . want . . .

My hand found the hardening tips of your breasts and you shuddered. I pressed my face into your neck and felt your blood, warm and swift-flowing beneath the skin, beat against my mouth. I wanted, not to devour you, but to absorb you, to become with you a single thing, naked and indivisible. You pulled away, but when I did not loose my grip on your waist, you leaned back towards me and your leg lifted beneath your heavy skirt so that you could press yourself against me. You turned your head and your mouth moved, wet against my ear.

You are breathing loud, too . . . I whispered. I could hardly speak.

Indeed, your panting seemed almost to hum through the bark of the tree at our backs. I felt it in my bones, a tickling buzz that began to make me itch. You lifted your head in surprise.

CHILLLLDRENNNN . . . OF . . . ADAMMMM.

You shrieked, Miranda, as well you might have. I do not know what I did or said. The voice was the drone of the wasp nest grown louder than any mortal voice, rumbling through the valley, the words understandable yet still horribly insectile.

Chillldrennn of Adammm, the voice said again, softer and more human this time. I looked up, flinching. The bird was perched atop the parchment globe of the nest, staring down at us. The squirrel clung to a lower branch, tufted ears cocked forward. *Do not fearrrr . . . I mean no harrrrmmm . . .*

What . . . where are you? Who speaks? you demanded, holding your hands across your breasts, all horrified modesty before a squirrel and a bird. I sat, stunned and terribly confused. What had happened to my afternoon, my love, my personal and secret valley?

I ammm a prrrrisonerrr inn the tree. As the voice spoke, the wasp nest trembled with each word. Its speech was swiftly becoming less unnatural, as though it learned with every passing moment. *I am a prisoner. Help me!*

Before I could stop you, Miranda, you had scrambled to your feet. I crawled along after you like a beast, too stupefied even to stand.

Do not tell your father! I shouted. *It cannot hurt us. It is my secret . . .* our *secret. Come back. Miranda!*

But you only hurried away up the valley. I paused, torn, then sprang away after you, leaving the tree or nest or whatever it was still moaning to itself at the base of the meadow.

I caught you at the hedge and tried to take your hand, but you turned, eyes rolling with anger or fear or both, and shoved me full in the chest, toppling me over into the thorns. I took a long, painful time extricating myself, and was crisscrossed with bloody weals when I had finished. The sun was beginning to set as I limped back to the house.

You were nowhere to be found, but the door to Prospero's room was shut.

All the misery I had suffered until then was as nothing to what came after. And it was you, Miranda, to whom I never did any harm, to whom I brought only love and admiration, who pushed me into the trap and then toppled the stone onto me.

If you had only told your father about the mysterious voice, things would have been bad enough, but you told him far more, enough to set his heart against me forever. Perhaps it was in guilty fear because you had left his side, or in shamed explanation of your soiled and torn clothing, for you had not been so careful passing through the thorns on the way out. Perhaps it was fear of something deeper, something in your own blood that had responded to my fumblings. Whatever drove you, you did what you should not have done: you made me your scapegoat.

Ill as he was, your father emerged that night from his room in a monstrous rage, a fury as powerful and terrifying as a hurricano-storm. Before the first words of explanation had passed my lips, he brought his staff down across my back and hammered me to the ground. That staff was more than a walking-stick; it had been woven about with many of your father's spells, and hung with talismans, but it had also been cured and polished with various of his strange concoctions until it was as hard as stone.

He proceeded then to beat me almost to death, smashing at my head and limbs and ribs as I lay curled on the floor, ranting as he did so that I had tried to defile his daughter, that I was a vile, vile beast, that the heavens would applaud him if he were to gut me like a slaughtered deer and hang me over the fire.

I almost wished he *would* kill me, which would at least have brought a quick end to my sufferings. As it was, only a shambling crawl for the door as he stood, panting with exhaustion, saved me. Bleeding with new wounds and the earlier thorn-spites, my bones grating inside me like broken crockery, I dragged myself into the trees and pulled such leaves as I could find over me, then sank into black insensibility.

You came to me with water sometime the next day, Miranda. I remember a break in the darkness during which I smelled you and felt the touch of something cool on my lips. In my fevered dreams I thought you had come to plead forgiveness, and were covering me in caresses, but when I woke again I was still alone in my nest of bloodied forest-tangle. The nightmares, the pain, were worse than what had followed the sow's attack.

Well you might shrink back against your soft bed, Miranda, for my anger still burns white-hot! Do you see this hand? Yes, it is strong – strong enough to deal with you in an instant – but the fingers are bent, crimped. Perhaps I was never beautiful, but as Nature or your God first made me, I was not crooked!

I could not walk again for several days, and all that

kept me alive were some small offerings you stole for me from your father's table. But I could not be grateful. Who had brought me to this? Who had traded my innocence for her own benefit?

As I slowly recovered, your father was all but oblivious to the injuries he had administered to his servant — the servant he had once treated like a son. Fresh smokes rose from the house's chimney, and a candle burned in his window every night until nearly dawn.

When a moon had bloomed and withered, and I was capable of limping in search of my own meals — and no longer deigned to take charity from you, my traitorous Miranda — I still kept away from the house, but like a phantom I haunted its outskirts. One day I saw from my hiding-place a strange thing: with you walking behind him, burdened with a sack, your father set out, dressed in his most impressive robes of black and silver, carrying the staff that had lately taken such a toll of my flesh.

The procession of two — three in truth, since I stole along behind in the forest fringe, a shadowy form hunched by ill-knit bones and stiffened limbs — made its way down one hillside and through the trees, then up into another set of hills. I was not surprised to see that the valley shielded by thorns was the destination. But of course it was shielded no longer, and Prospero marched through the wrack of the burning like a conqueror.

He made his way without hesitation to the tree at

the valley's base; you lagged behind, showing every appearance of reluctance about approaching the spot. From a distance I could not hear all that happened, but I could see your father speaking up into the branches of the tree, and listening to whatever replies came. After a while he built a ring of stones and set a fire in it, then sat down, bidding you do the same. Afternoon turned into evening, and when the first star crept into the sky he rose again and called for you to bring him his books.

A long time he chanted, slowly turning the pages of his volumes, stopping only to lift his staff and draw invisible shapes in the air. His voice grew louder, almost triumphant. The tree shuddered, as though gripped by a strong wind, but no other tree in the valley moved. My ears began to hurt, as when I dived too deep in the sea. Then, with a crack louder than thunder, the ancient pine tree split into flinders. A great shower of sparks leaped from the shattered tree and whirled in the air; I thought the wasps in their nest had caught fire and flew in dying circles. The sparks grew into a tower of flickering light which billowed in the winds that now rushed through the small valley, but though I quailed and you covered your eyes, your father spread his arms wide and shouted.

I name you and bind you, Ariel the Fallen! Beneath Solomon's Seal, your fealty belongs to me!

The pillared sparks bloomed for a moment, spreading outward, then fell back on themselves and became a figure of almost unseeable brightness, a white flame in a man's shape. The voice, still buzzingly inhuman, crawled into my ears as though the shining thing stood beside me.

Ariel I am. You have freed me from my prison, Child of Adam. I will do your bidding.

I fled into the forest in horror. Now I knew what my mother had fought on the beach before I was born. I had foolishly bared my soul to the thing that she had defeated and imprisoned, and now it had been loosed.

Caliban was no longer the favourite servant.

In SLAVERY

FOR SOME DAYS, perhaps weeks, I wandered the less accessible places of my island, aching and friendless. Many nights I lay curled beneath the leaves or in the hollows between rocks and wept to think of the home I had lost, the friends who had turned against me.

I was determined to make my own way. If Prospero was too strong for me, if he had gained a new servitor, if his daughter hated me enough to betray me, then I would leave them their field of victory. The island was small, but there were still places of retreat, isolated spots where I could feed myself and nurse my hurts in peace and never again glimpse your beautiful, treacherous face.

But of course it was not to be.

I was crouching in a hidden cove eating a fish when suddenly I was transfixed by a terrible pain. I roared in agony and dropped the remains of my meal onto the sand. My guts felt as though they were

twisted by some invisible hand; within moments I
vomited up the portion I had already swallowed.
Certain that I had eaten some kind of poison, I
stumbled towards the nearest fresh water spring,
but every step seemed to increase my misery. I
turned in circles as the pains griped me, and
perceived that when I turned towards one particular
direction, the sickness seemed less. Blind self-
preservation kept me facing that way, and when I
took a step forward, the pain eased a little more.

As long as I moved forward, and in one direction
only, the wrenching of my guts diminished. I found
myself staggering up from the beach and into the
forest. After a few hundred steps I saw where I was
headed and swerved aside, but the agony returned
so strongly that I was knocked to the earth. I crawled
forward, once more headed towards Prospero's
house, and my suffering eased a bit. At last I was
able to stand up, but I could not cease moving
forward or the pain quickly returned.

All the sounds of the forest seemed harsh and
unpleasant, sour birdsong, the itching hiss of grass
beneath my feet, but before long an even more
unmelodious noise fell upon my ears.

Greetings, little witchspawn.

He, she — whatever it was — sat on a slender
branch which bowed only slightly beneath its
weight. It wore the shape of a slender child, but the
pale body was curiously featureless, un-nippled,
un-naveled; the eyes might have been black holes,

but for a faint glint on their surface. Along its arms and the top of its head, and also in the place where it had neither the member of a man nor the crease of a woman, were fletchings of tiny feathers that seemed to glow and smoke at their edges.

It is you who tortures me, I gasped. *I should have known.*

And if I did, who can blame me? Its buzzing voice had reached its apex of humanity, and still fell short of anything homely. *You are the whelp of the creature that imprisoned me. But as it happens, I am merely the extended hand of my master . . . and yours. Prospero wishes to see you.*

I will not go. I sank to the ground, but instantly leapt up again. My skin burned in a thousand, thousand places, as though I were covered in swarmings ants.

Of course you will go. Follow me, monster.

And it sprang into the air, half-transparent, and danced on nothingness. It floated ahead of me like a fleck of fire-ash, singing.

> *Suck, bee; wasp, sting.*
> *Make a home for everything.*
> *Fishes in the silted deep*
> *Sniff the sailors fast asleep.*
> *Sting, bee; wasp, kiss.*
> *Make me now a part of this.*
> *Birds with crack-glass yellow eyes*
> *Chase the echo through the skies . . .*

Moaning, scratching myself bloody, I shambled in its wake.

Prospero was sitting in front of the house, holding something in his hands. I collapsed on the ground before him, gasping for breath. The stinging became weaker and the twisting of my guts eased, but I was too beaten down to move, much less attempt either to escape or to attack my tormentor.

I expected too much of you, Prospero rumbled. Wincing, I slowly lifted my head until I could see his cold eyes.

I have done you no wrong . . .

Wrong? He laughed, a dry rattle. I saw Ariel skim past him and alight on the roof, then sit cross-legged to watch. *You are alive this moment by virtue of my daughter's pleading, only. I taught her too much kindness, as I taught you too much pride.*

As he spoke, I saw his daughter's face in the window – your face. You looked pale and fearful, but that did not surprise me: it was not hard for me to imagine what you must see, the horror I had become, made crooked by your father's blows, covered with mud and bleeding weals.

I am not so low, I growled. *Nor am I only what you have made me . . .*

Silence! Prospero stood. *I call you unteachable, but you must needs prove me wrong. There is work for you. Ariel is too valuable a servant to waste on petty chores, and . . .*

And my time of servitude is limited, the crowing voice pealed from the rooftop.

. . . And I have a more important task for Ariel to undertake, Prospero finished, darting a swift glance towards the thatch. *One that will right an evil long unavenged. So you will be allowed to live, and to repay the debt you owe me.*

Debt? I groaned. *Repay? This was* my *island. I lived here as king.*

You lived here as a beast lives. I tried to change that. I failed.

I was a friend to your daughter, curse you — a true friend!

Prospero said nothing, but nodded as if in regretful acquiescence. A moment later I was again wracked with horrible pain until I ground my face against the earth and howled.

A true friend? he said at last. *A true friend to my pure Miranda? Look up, beast. Look here.*

Knowing the torture would begin again if I resisted, I did as he bade me. He lifted his hand to show what he had been holding. It was a doll, a marvellously formed figure of a young girl made from white clay, with a tuft of golden-brown hair. Prospero set it on the ground and sprinkled it with something. It began to dance prettily.

A lovely thing, isn't she? His face belied his soft words. *And now we shall make her a friend . . . but this island offers only poor material.*

So saying, he bent again and clawed up a handful

of mud, then squeezed it into a vaguely manlike form, a gross, misshapen lump with crooked arms and legs. When he had sprinkled it with the dust and set it down, it began to drag itself after the little dancer, oozing and crumbling as it went. The girl-puppet paused for a moment, as if staring. The lump hunched towards her, then began to do a crude dance of its own. Each step made a squelching noise.

Good, good! An inhuman cackle of laughter echoed down from the roof-thatch. *I was told you dance, Caliban. I witnessed a little of your grace on the journey here.*

Do you see? Prospero had adopted the patient tone of one who must repeat a lesson for a foolish student. *I tried to make it a man, but the dirt here is not sufficient to the task.*

The mud-thing now ceased dancing and hobbled towards the other doll, then caught her in its uneven arms. The little clay girl struggled, but could not pull free. Everywhere the mud-thing touched her, it streaked her with dark smears.

It cannot be allowed, Prospero said. He reached down and pulled the slender dancer free, then stamped the other beneath his heel. Although my eyes had filled with helpless tears, I thought I saw a bubble bulge and then gape in its head—like a screaming mouth before it was crushed into oblivion.

You see? It is hopeless. Some things cannot be improved, though we kill ourselves with trying. Now go to your room, or Ariel will convey you there in a way you do not like.

Weeping, I crawled across the earth towards the shed that had been my home. I passed within a hand's-breadth of Prospero's black boots. He did not move.

His daughter's face had vanished from the window.

As I dragged myself over the doorstep, I heard Ariel crowing:

> *Ban, Ban, Caliban!*
> *Not much of a monster,*
> *Much less of a man!*

And there you lie, Miranda, with a look of indignant, threatened innocence drawn across your face like a veil. Innocence? Even had you shown me nothing but kindness, even had you been as loyal as streams are to the ocean, always returning, how could I let you live, who have seen me on that day?

Do not speak! At this moment I cannot bear to hear your lying voice. What would you tell me? That you begged your father on my behalf? That you softened his treatment of me by your quiet urgings, your daughterly coaxing? Nothing, nothing, and less than nothing! Such petty help was dust in a tempest wind. I denounce you, Miranda! If there was ever a thimbleful of justice in you, you should have bent over me to shield me from his blows; you should have flung yourself onto the jagged rocks at the ocean's edge rather than watch him abuse me as he did. If ever *I* had a child, and she was as weakly treacherous as you, I would bury her in a deep hole while she still breathed.

You knew, Miranda. You knew I had done no wrong, and yet you stood by and watched as everything I had was stolen from me and my face was pressed against the hard stone. And yet, in the days afterward, you thought that an occasional kind word as I fetched and carried, an incident or two of lukewarm protest when your father insulted and punished me, a murmur of distaste when Ariel tormented me almost to madness, were enough to redeem your sins. May your God damn you, woman! There is no sin more vile than half-hearted, insincere protestation. Damnation to you!

And yet I still loved you. Riddle that, spirits of my island. Like a torn scarf which once had been good enough for best wear, but now is used to sop up stains, you cast me aside . . . but I still loved you. And do, woman, and do.

There is hard work in hatred, Miranda. Love is a slightly less demanding task. Ah, but when you love *and* hate at the same time, with both feelings bent on the same object, one gives strength to the other. Thus it is possible to play a long game.

I hear the cry of the gate-watch outside. Our time begins to run short, so I will spare you a recital of the delights that each day in your father's service brought me . . . but perhaps that is just as well: I fear that the pleasure of reliving those years might cause me to end our evening precipitately. I am stuffed full of dark thoughts, Miranda. Tonight they are over-spilling . . . but measure, measure, Caliban. All in its place.

I called Prospero 'Master'. I called you 'Mistress'. Even when we were alone, I called you that, for fear that invisible Ariel might lurk, listening. Ah, were there some way I could take my just revenge on that hell-sprite I might, as a barter, even renounce what I plan for you. Still, even for a chance at Ariel I would not have given over my plans for your father. No, Prospero was the chiefest demon, and I curse him through Death for eluding me.

As some take their hours of leisure walking or singing, the creature Ariel delighted in following me about, filling my day with tricks and taunts and other persecutions. As long as your father wanted my strong, bent back, Ariel was not allowed to kill me, but it made my days a misery. It flew around my head in the shape of a wasp, stinging me until tears of helpless rage ran down my face. It sang to me songs of my mother's putrefaction, chirping sweetly of her eyes falling into her skull and her flesh becoming sodden muck — even that she and the murdered sow had joined together beneath the earth as a sort of rotting family, that even my dead mother had forgotten me. And it taunted me about you,

Miranda, how it taunted me! It tormented me with lies, claiming I had stalked you by the pool and had planned to ravish you, saying the bird had seen me at it. It whispered back to me all those endearments which I had been foolish enough to cry to what I thought was empty air, and which it had heard through the ears of the squirrel I called Pest. Pestilence and plague, indeed. Squirrel-ear, bird-eye, tongue of buzzing wasps: imprisoned in the tree, Ariel had made for itself everything but a heart.

Even when it was not plaguing me with nips and bites and burning pains on my foot-soles, Ariel could not leave me alone. It perched in the trees above my head and yammered in its scratchy voice until I thought I would shriek. It told me long, maddening stories of its origins, each one different. Once it claimed it was the shade of a man my mother had murdered with her witchcraft. Another time it claimed to be a fallen angel, one of Lucifer's rebel army. Other times it sang strange songs of waking first in the boiling heart of a volcano, a spirit of fire.

A fairy, a demon, an orphan of another spinning world, every tale different, still the creature prattled on. I did not care, and do not now. If your God is real, and He created a universe with things like Ariel in it, He is a master like Prospero was: He deserves to be overthrown and smothered in His bedclothes.

The days of my servitude wore on. I got nothing but harsh words from your father, but those were surprisingly few. He was playing some deep game, now that he commanded a power such as Ariel, and he was seldom away from his books. Even you did not see him often . . . nor, I think, suspect what he planned. In some ways, you were as much his slave as I. There is no absolution for you there, Miranda, but there is perhaps some mitigation when you stand before whatever judgement will follow mine. And both now loom very near.

If ever I truly was an animal – and the spark within me shouts protest against the thought – it was in that time. Before you came to my island, I had been ignorant of speech, but I had known hope and joy and simple pleasure in the fact of my life; now all those things were gone. I lost sight of everything but beastlike plodding, my spirit mired in sullen misery. I was truly the mud-man.

I cannot speak of it. Even now, I cannot speak of it. To hobble back and forth every day, crooked and soiled, beneath your pitying eyes . . . I would have killed you and your pity a dozen times, but I feared what your father would then have Ariel do to me. As miserable as my life was, it was my only remaining possession, and so I added to my own self-hatred with a tally of cowardice. I could only hope that somehow, impossibly, deliverance might come, but could not imagine how such a thing might happen.

And you, Miranda, were only a little more happily disposed. You were bait for the trap your father was building. But I did not know that – *you* did not know it – and so I deemed you just as malicious as your father.

Prospero held himself a good man who had been poorly used. Even should we set aside his vicious treatment of me, Miranda, does putting the terror of a watery death into his enemies – achieved at what he felt was the petty cost of drowning a few dozen sailors – sound like the action of a good man? Does baiting with his daughter's virtue a snare to recatch his dukedom sound like goodness? And the selling of that daughter to his old enemy to enable his own resumption of power? I am sure you thought your swift love for Ferdinand genuine, but it was the last thing needed for Prospero's complete triumph: he must have known, even planned, that it would happen. How could you fail to love a tall, handsome young stranger? What comparison did you have but crippled, muddy Caliban?

The king's ship came to the island, lured and then sunk by some sorcery of your father and his hellish servant – a spell long in preparation, swift and terrifying in execution.

I knew nothing of it, but as Ariel worked its magics, painting storms across the sky that seemed to roar like a thousand monsters and scorch the very fabric of heaven, I hid cowering in a grotto by the seashore, and there was almost drowned by the high-leaping waves. Had that happened, perhaps you would be smiling and dandling your children even this moment, soothing their night-terrors instead of facing one of your own. Certainly no tears would have been wasted on Caliban: by the time old Alonso and his liegemen were drawn to the island, I had already served my purpose. But I escaped the waves and fought my way up the cliff-face into the hills above, weeping in fear as the thunder cracked on, louder than any I had ever heard. On either side of me trees were split by jagged lightning-thrusts and left as smoking husks, a hundred replicas of the riven pine from which Ariel had sprung.

Thus I did not see the ship's survivors coming to land. When the first of them happened upon me, I was astonished, and thought them spirits of the storm, perhaps even brothers to Ariel. I cowered in the undergrowth beside the path, but they were as frightened by me as I of them.

Poor Stephano and Trinculo. Unlucky men, to have made such a doomful friend as me!

Oh, the lies your father later told you, Miranda, and which you hurried to believe. He told you that those sailors and I plotted some murderous rebellion, that only his wits and Ariel's magics saved you and him from death. Lies, lies, lies!

They were rough fellows, those two, but honest withal. When I spoke, thinking to placate these new tormentors, they thought me a prodigy, a sport of nature. *An ape that speaks!* one said, and the other nodded. When I told them I was the son of an exile, and that I had been enslaved by a later arrival, they were astounded, but when I told them who it was who had enslaved me they were less surprised.

Prospero the warlock. That name is well known, and well feared, said Stephano. *His dark arts were a danger to Milan, and so he was driven thence.*

Then they feared for the safety of their king, who had earned Prospero's hatred by supporting the wizard's brother in his overthrow. They had been sent to explore the island and find help if possible, but now they gave over their task and hurried back towards the beach where the ship's passengers had floundered ashore, bidding me accompany them and promising me food and protection from my master. For the first time, I dared to hope that my life might be changed.

Hope is a cruelty even Ariel had not mastered. Foolish Caliban. Foolish, foolish mud-man!

The king and his party were gone, the beach empty but for a single sandy corpse, one of the sailors cast overboard by the storm who had finally washed onto the shore. I stared at his bulging, sightless eyes as Stephano and Trinculo cursed their luck. He was another of your father's victims, Miranda. I do not even know his name, but he had curly dark hair and wore a cross carved from ivory around his neck. In some other world I may see him, and if so, I will tell him that there is no justice on this earth, where the games of some cause the deaths of men they do not know. I have not spent long among your kind, Miranda. Perhaps he knew this even before the sea took him.

We hurried on in pursuit of King Alonso, but Ariel's storm-spell had left webs of magic everywhere; my familiar island had become a maze of confusion. False trails, misleading sounds and sourceless lights, several times a shimmer of music from nowhere, led us through the forest tracks for hours, but never any closer to our goal. We grew tired and dropped for a while to sleep a fitful sleep before wakening and staggering on.

We arrived at the house on the hillside at last, to discover that the game was played, the story told, and we three but comic afterthoughts. Ariel laid a further spell on Stephano and Trinculo that made their weariness seem drunken foolery, thus to discredit their warnings. King Alonso, bemused by your father's magics, had made a great apology and renunciation, and now stood beaming like a drunkard himself, clasping Prospero's hand and proclaiming that all wrongs would be righted, all crimes punished. And since Antonio, your father's usurping brother, had been one of those drowned, there was conveniently no other claimant to Milan's throne.

But even as I swayed, blinking at what for me was an almost incomprehensibly vast crowd of other people, something I had never thought to see, I began to realise that the wrongs *I* had suffered would go very much unrighted.

Then you appeared, Miranda, clutching at a boy with a face pale as goat's milk, and an expression no cleverer than would adorn a goat's front. But it was not the expression on *his* face that caused my heart to tumble down into a dark hole.

The king had apparently thought his cream-faced son dead, and made loud cries of astonishment. He embraced him, then wonderingly embraced you as well.

This is my Miranda, his son Ferdinand told him. *She will be my wife. She is beautiful and kind, and is properly a maiden.*

Your daughter, Duke Prosper? Alonso asked in some surprise.

Aye, and pure, every inch, answered your father. *Fit bride for a prince. If it is your pleasure they should wed, we may make the return voyage a wedding-progress.*

Alas, declared Alonso, *our ship is sunk. We are marooned, all.*

Prospero nodded, smiling deep in his beard.

There was other talk then, but I did not hear it. The sight of you mooning at Ferdinand was a knife in my eye. My ears filled with a terrible rushing, as though Ariel had resummoned the storm; I fell to my knees between Stephano and Trinculo and gave out a great cry. But no one paid any attention. The spell-dazzled pair beside me had not the wits, and all the others were too full of questions and celebration. I groaned again, and would not have been surprised had my heart split in my breast and killed me. But Fate had in mind for me a longer spell of suffering.

There was a great festival that night. Ariel conjured a magic banquet, but with freedom only hours away, I wonder how much attention the hell-sprite gave to its work: some of the viands turned ghostly and then vanished entirely before they could be eaten. As for the rest of the meal, one might wonder how filling it was.

In any case, it all mattered little to me. Prospero bade me serve, but I would not. After Stephano and Trinculo had been called rebels and clapped in chains by their ungrateful ruler, I no longer cared what might happen, and lay all evening as one dead near the front door of the house, refusing to get up. Prospero was angry, but did not have Ariel harry me into service. Perhaps he feared to show his new allies how his will was usually accomplished.

You, Miranda, you had eyes for nothing but your new love, that odious princeling with whom, I suspect, your father had long planned to breed you like a heifer. Ferdinand paddled at your neck and fed you with his own fingers – an affection that I have no doubt lasted only slightly longer than Ariel's repast – while your sire looked on, beaming his approval. Your father's onetime toady Gonzalo, now restored to his service, proposed salutation after salutation, both to Prosper and Alonso, bidding Heaven smile on the binding-up of old hurts and the union of two such noble families.

And they all stand upon my neck, I groaned in the shadows. *Ban, Ban, Caliban.*

At the end of the meal, Ariel — still invisible to any save me and Prospero, since you had eyes only for Prince Whey-face — flew into the sky at your father's whispered command.

Behold, your father cried aloud. *The last of my magics, but not the least!* He waved his staff.

Instantly there flew across the face of the moon a streak of fire, which widened into a blazing sheet, then became the image of a ship. The king's vessel, etched in lines of flame, burned against the velvety night, rocking and wallowing as though it might sink.

Miracle of miracles, cried Alfonso, *it is the very picture of the tempest that wrecked us!*

The fiery boat sank in burning waves and tiny flaming figures swam away from it. Then, as the onlookers gasped and pointed, the ship faded in a drizzle of sparks. It was only when the last of the glowing drops had vanished that we could see a great shimmer of light rising above the trees, a subtler radiance that seemed to have it source in the ocean far below us.

What is this, Duke Prospero? cried young Ferdinand, clasping you to him with a great show of protectiveness. *Have your fire-magics set the forest ablaze?*

After me and you will discover, your father said, and set out down the hillside, his staff suddenly burning at its tip like a torch.

The company rose and followed. I would have remained where I lay huddled, having no desire to see anything more, half-hoping that the forest had indeed caught fire and would soon burn me and the island and everyone else to mute ash. But of course, Ariel and Prospero intended that *all* should witness their final triumph, and I was soon chivvied down the hill after the others, pursued by invisible biters.

We stopped upon the beach, all but me staring in awe at the ocean, which shone from below with a great pearly-green light, as though the absent sun were reborn in its depths. The glow spread. Then, with a great tumult of waters, the king's true ship rose up through the fathoms until it bobbed atop the waves. Seablood ran off it in great sheets. Blue fire leaped among the masts. Here and there a waxy corpse dangled in the rigging.

Your ship is raised, Prospero told the king, and bowed as one who has done a modest but significant favour. *We may sail back to Naples. Justly, I am once more become Milan absolute, and so I abjure further magics.*

As he spoke, he scratched something in the sand – marks the others were too thunderstruck by the appearance of the ship to notice. But I, perhaps alone, heard a great buzzing peal of laughter echo across the strand, then saw some flaming thing leap from the pinnacle of the mainmast and vanish in a shower of yellow sparks. An instant later something hurtled past me, knocking me from my feet with the wind of its passage, leaving only the echo of a few mocking words behind as it flew to freedom.

> *Find a new master*
> *Get a new man!*

As I lay panting in the dirt, you detached yourself from the milling company and made your way toward me. You were dressed in your finest clothes; I wore only rags and mud, my head garlanded with briar-tangles.

Caliban?

I turned my face away.

My father is a strict man, but not a cruel one. I have told him that your rebellion was only foolishness. He has decided to forgive you.

I clenched my fist but said nothing. I wished only for you to go away and leave me in peace.

You will be punished no further. And you will have your island back again, as you wished, for we are returning to Naples with King Alonso.

You sensed the anger in my silence, for you said: *Can you not be happy for me, Caliban? I love Ferdinand truly, and soon I will see again the place I was born. It will be as a new world to me!*

I stared at the pale-faced, chattering company you

had left down on the beach, vile Prospero, senile Alonso, and all the rest.

O, brave new world it must be, I growled, *that has such creatures in it. Go to it, you. It will be a fit place for your like.*

You turned away then, and until I appeared in your bedroom tonight, we exchanged no more words. But I was not to be allowed even my final furious mourning. As I crawled away into the forest, I heard footfalls behind me. Your father's black boots stepped in front of me, forcing me to halt.

I have dealt harshly with you in the past, Caliban, but it was for your own betterment. Now I leave you to your future and your freedom.

Go away, you madman! I cried. *Let me be!*

He hesitated, then turned and paced back toward the beach. I crouched, sobbing, and heard him stop again. I lowered my head and tried to cover my ears, but could not shut out his last, terrible words.

In my way, little savage, I loved you once.

And then he was gone.

PART the THIRD
Naples: Morning

His EXIT

SHE STRUGGLED, BUT the dark fingers did not relax their grip. His face had moved close to her ear as though he might kiss it, or bite it. His voice had not risen above a whisper for some time.

Miranda heaved, mouth gaping and eyes wide. Abruptly, the hand upon her neck relaxed. She coughed, rubbing at the red marks he had left on her skin.

'You were not listening properly,' he said. 'I am sorry if I hurt you.'

She gasped in startled anger, then winced at the pain it caused. 'You apologise for hurting, when at any moment now you will kill me? You are mad.'

He lidded his yellow eyes for a moment. 'I did not come to torture you, my Miranda, but to make you hear. What I do last will be swift and with little pain. I promise that.'

She slumped back among the bedclothes. 'It is . . . hard to hear this. Hurry and do what you will.'

'I have not finished.' He held his great, gnarled fingers before him, as though surprised to find himself attached to them. 'There is a little to tell, still.

'You and the rest sailed with the morning's sun. You returned with Prospero to Milan until the preparations for your marriage to the prince were finished. Then, as old Alonso grew feeble, you followed your new lord and master to his family home in Naples. You know this already, of course, but I had to discover it in pieces, in fragments of conversation. I learned much from talking with old sailors and others who do not begrudge a fellow-drinker his ugliness if the ugly one is paying for the wine . . . or stealing it, as the case may be.

'What you do not know, and did not care about, is what *I* did in those years . . .

'With my heart smashed inside me like a dropped egg, I at first could think of nothing. I fed myself, I wandered up and down the empty beach, I sang to the unlistening sky. But as the months turned into a year, and then years, the silence began to smother me.

'You might think it odd to describe the island as a silent place, with its shrill monkey-chatter and screech of birds, noises of wind and weather, the perpetual rumble of the sea. But I had become used to the sound of human speech, Miranda. There is no silence so frightening as that which rises up when one's own voice stops and there is no one to listen or to care.

'Twenty years, Miranda. Twenty unspeakably long years. There were times, I swear, when I even longed to hear the hideous buzzing of Ariel again, just to prove that I had not dreamed it all . . . just to break the silence. Your father claimed to have given me my freedom. By the spirits! Even had he any right to have taken it at all, he replaced my slavery with a penance worse by far.

'You two took my innocence from me. You stole my island, but not merely the physical fact of it. With your words, your names, your ideas, even your very presence, you took the place I had lived all my life and set it somewhere beyond my reach. During the two decades of miserable, solitary exile after you sailed away, the island never again felt like the home it had been. Everything now had a name, and each name was an artefact of Prosper and Miranda. Every place was somewhere we had experienced together, and contained some ghost of your father or you. Even the way I thought about my childhood home was irretrievably changed. You *stole* it from me – damn you, damn you, damn you! You took the only things I possessed – my island, my heart, my life – and sailed away.

'And perhaps cruellest of all, you infected me with speech, then uncaringly left me to live out my life in empty, lonely silence.

'Do you wonder then that when a ship finally anchored off the coast, and men came in search of fruit and meat and fresh water, that I swam out by night and clambered aboard? It was not easy to hide for the whole of that long sea-voyage, but I can be fearfully stealthy when I wish to. After twenty years, I had only one happy thought left, and that was vengeance.

'Do you wonder that I made my way to Milan in search of your father, determined to slay him with these hands? My quest was not a simple one, Miranda – I knew nothing much of your world when the ship brought me to your shores, and know only a little more now – but there is a fire burning in me that will not be quenched. But in everything that I did, I offered no harm to those who did not wish to harm me, and I killed no one. How could I, after all my suffering, use other innocents after the fashion of the sailor your father drowned and left upon the beach?

'Searching first for your father, then you, I learned enough of this world to know I want no part of it. The pictures in your father's books lied. It is not beautiful and strange; it is foul. It is deadly, at least to me. Books lie. A drawing of a serpent does not describe what its venom feels like scalding in your veins.

'So when I have finished what I came to do tonight, I will do my best to make my way back to my island. For all the corruption you brought to it, it is still a sort of home – the only one *I* will ever know. I know which ships will take me there, and if I must once again hide among stinking fish for my passage, what is that to a monster?'

He paused, breathing hard. His hands had once more strayed to Miranda's shoulders, and now sat like great spiders on either side of her throat.

'It will be day soon. The guards must have begun looking for their missing counterpart. Your father escaped me, pretty Miranda, but you have not.'

A tear ran down her face and into the hollow beneath her chin. 'And so you will slay me? After all your talking?' There seemed little fear in her voice, but a great weariness.

'If there is a speck of justice in all the emptiness of the world, I can do nothing else,' he said. 'I regret that it should be so, but . . .'

His fingers closed upon her neck and she let out a little gasp. For a moment the long muscles in his arms bunched beneath the fur. From somewhere in the room there came a soft fluttering noise, like a trapped bird beating with its wings against a curtain. Her hands reached up and closed around his wrists, but gently.

'No. I . . . cannot do it this way.' He pulled a cushion from beneath her head. 'I thought that I would wish to see your eyes at the end, Miranda, but I find I do not.' He moved onto the edge of the bed, leaning his heavy body across her, pinioning her arms and legs, then lowered the cushion towards her face. 'I will hold another memory of you, I think . . .'

'*Stop!*'

The voice was muffled. The tapestry that hung beside the door billowed, then one edge sagged and tore free as a pale figure fought its way loose. 'No, please, do not hurt her!'

The monster stared, amazed. The young girl hurried forward and pulled his unresisting hand from the cushion, then lifted it from Miranda's head and buried her own face in her mother's breast, sobbing.

'Giulietta,' her mother gasped. For the first time in some long while feeling had returned to her voice. 'Oh, merciful Lord, what are you doing here? Run away, daughter, *run*!'

A dark arm stretched. The monster's hand closed on Giulietta's neck . . . but gently. 'How long have you listened?' he growled.

'Is it true?' Giulietta demanded, lifting her tear-stained eyes to her mother's. 'Is it all true?'

Miranda too was weeping. 'Oh, sweet God, why did you come?'

'I . . . could not sleep. Bad dreams. I came to talk to you, then hid when I heard voices. Is it *true*, Mother? What he said?'

Her mother could not reply.

'Enough.' He tightened his grip, pulling the girl upright. His voice was flat and harsh. 'I would not slay an innocent, but the tears of this piglet will not prevent the execution of the sow. I am sorry you should see this, child, but you have earned it as penalty for your spying.'

Miranda sat up, striking uselessly at Caliban's arms. 'Do not hurt her! She has done nothing!'

'As *I* did nothing, but still was punished, you stupid woman?' he growled. 'Or as *you* did nothing, when your father and Ariel tormented me, day in and day out? There are many sorts of nothing.' He pushed her roughly back down. 'But I said I would not slay her. Do you never listen? Or have so many years of living with lies made you deaf to the truth?' He raised the cushion over her head. 'She has heard what you did to me, now she will see a rough justice done. Afterward she will join that useless old guard in forced slumber.'

Miranda closed her eyes. 'Oh, God, then let it be. Do not hurt her, Caliban. As you said, she is an innocent.'

Giulietta twisted in his grip. 'Do not kill my mother.'

'She can atone no other way, child.'

'Take me instead.'

'No!' Miranda again began to struggle.

'Silence, both of you!' He pulled the daughter up and shoved her to one side. 'You have not listened well either, child, if you think I would slay you or even harm you. Go, run – I will be done with this before you can bring help.'

'No, take me with you. Spare my mother. *Take me away with you!*'

At her words a silence descended on the room, an expanding instant in which the very flame of the candle seemed to freeze into immobility.

His eyes narrowed. 'What are you saying? What madness ... .'

'Take me back to your island. I will live there with you.' She sat up, rubbing the tears from her face. 'There is nothing for me here but a marriage to fat Renato Ursino and a life spent raising his babies. Take me to live on your island. I will be *your* servant. The debt will be repaid.'

'No, Giulietta, my little rabbit, you are mad, you do not know what you are saying! He is . . . he is a beast! You do not know what you say!' Claw-fingered, Miranda reached out for her daughter, but the girl slipped from the bed and stood up.

'But I do.' She turned and fixed him with her gaze, but her lip trembled. 'I do. If you will spare my mother, I will be your companion. I have listened to you all the night long. I think you are no monster, but a man.' She spread her hands, imploring. '*I have listened.* I will go with you.'

'Do not heed her, Caliban,' Miranda pleaded. 'Slay me if you must! But do not take her. She is only a foolish child – she knows not what she says!'

As the great dark head swivelled from daughter to mother, there was a clatter in the courtyard below, followed by the muffled voices of men.

'I wonder,' he said slowly. 'She is much like you – before your father's grasping hands squeezed the life from you.' He turned back to Giulietta. 'You will be my companion, you say? It will not be easy. Just finding our way back to the island will take many moons, and the travelling will be hard. And life on the island is not as you might imagine it. You have lived in this great house all your life, been petted and kissed, gifted with soft clothes and fine meals. Even to spare your mother's life, it would be a heavy price for you to pay.'

She stared back at him, a touch of her grandfather's fierce glint in her eyes. 'I do it not to spare my mother's life . . . although of course I love her and would see her spared. I will go with you for my own sake. That is all.'

He threw back his head and laughed. 'Hah! Sacrifice, escape, revenge – or all three, perhaps? I think the island serpents would do well to stay out of your path, girl.' He fell silent as he considered, but voices could still be heard rising from the courtyard.

'Very well,' he said at last, then stood and gestured toward the large chests of Lebanon cedar that lined an alcove in the far wall. 'Find yourself some garments suitable for rough travelling. I am sure your mother has clothes to spare. Quick, now!'

The girl glanced at her mother for a moment, suddenly unsure, then moved like a sleepwalker toward the wardrobe.

He turned back to the bed, bent his crooked leg, and sketched a mocking bow. 'It seems your execution is stayed, my beautiful Miranda. Strangely, I find myself somewhat relieved.'

She fought with the entangling blankets, struggling to rise. 'But surely you do not . . . would not . . .'

'But I do. I will.'

'Please! You cannot be so cruel!' She stood and clutched the bedpost, swaying. 'Please! You cannot take my daughter from me!'

'And why not? You took almost the whole of my life from me. Besides, I came late to cruelty, and have much ground to make up on those who taught me.'

She lurched forward and caught at his arm. 'I did not mean you harm, Caliban! I did not understand how much pain you felt . . .'

'No? Then you were wilfully ignorant.'

'Perhaps!' Miranda began to weep. 'Yes! Yes, I was. But I was frightened! I was only a child, Caliban, only a child! I did not rejoice to see you mistreated, but how could I contradict my father?'

He peered at her for a moment, the muscles of his neck and arms tensed as though he held in, at cost, some great violence. But when he spoke his words were soft.

'And does it never end, then? Is darkness merely to be passed on, hand to hand, like a family heirloom?' He took her shoulders and pulled her toward him, until he held her almost as a lover might. She began to sag against him, but he kept her at a little distance. 'If God sends lightning to burn down your house, do you thank Him, praise Him, and live forever after in the ash and rubble? Or do you clean away the charred wrack and build a new house?'

'I . . . I do not understand you.'

'I think you do, Miranda. In some place, at some hour, responsibility must be taken at last.'

He gently pushed her away and moved toward the window, wrapping his cloak in several folds around his arm. She sank to her knees.

'Oh, God,' she groaned. 'So there is nothing I can do. You will take her away. I will lose my daughter.'

'It seems you have mostly lost her already. But yes, you will suffer, and you will regret. At least you have the faint consolation that she has made her own choice. That is more than nothing, is it not?'

Miranda did not reply. She covered her face with her hands.

'Come, young one,' he called. 'It is time. The guard has changed, and they will come to look for their missing comrade very soon.'

The girl let the lid of the chest fall shut. She wore a dark, heavy cloak and an expression of anxious resolution.

'Now?'

The monster nodded, then thrust his covered arm through the window panes, one after the other. What seemed an unending shower of glass tinkled onto a lower section of the roof. When he had finished, he carefully broke out the wooden cross-bars. A chill wind moved through the room; the candle-flame cast jittering shadows.

'You would do well to prepare a lie, Miranda,' he said. 'Otherwise, someone may be injured in the pursuit of us. I wish no harm to innocents, but I will never again let myself be captured and used like a beast.' His voice took on an edge of scorn. 'I think for one so versed in that city-art, falsification will not prove much of a challenge. In any case, you may tell them every bit of truth except that you know who the abductor is, and that you know where he is taking your daughter.'

He paused, regarding her where she crouched on the cold floor. 'Remember, Miranda, whether I am beast or man, you have made me what I am. I have no pity for you. But you are a mother, and even Caliban had one of those, so I will also tell you this . . .'

He moved to the window and beckoned to Giulietta. She hesitated, then ran and embraced Miranda, pressing her wet cheek against her mother's for a long moment before pulling free of her desperate grasp. A moment later she stood shivering beside the dark figure.

'Oh, God,' whispered Miranda. 'I wish . . . I wish . . .'

He raised his hand. 'Listen: I will treat her with exactly the same respect and kindness and love which I showed to you. I swear that by all the spirits of my island.' He looked down at the small shape beside him.

'So now we come to the test. If I am the monster you and your father made me out, then you should run and throw open the doors and shout for help this very instant. For if I am that brute, surely no promise of mine can be trusted, and you would be abandoning your beloved child to ravishment and murder.' He caught at Giulietta's arm, then slid out through the broken window. 'If I am what your father claimed, you are guiltless in anything you have done to me. If I am that beast, then everything I have said tonight is self-serving falsehood – a bad dream – and you can send your soldiers after me, to kill me and to bring back your daughter. You will sleep with an easy conscience.'

He helped the girl through the window, then effortlessly swept her up in one massive arm. Her cloak flapped in the wind. She seemed a little frightened now, but wrapped her arms around his neck and said nothing.

'If not, then give us until the candle burns down to escape.'

Miranda took her hands away from her face. Her skin was pale, her eyes red-rimmed.

'So, Prosper's daughter,' he murmured. 'So.' At such a distance from the candle-flame, little could be seen of him except the owlish gleam of his eyes. 'It has been a long night. Farewell.'

Miranda opened her mouth to say something, but before she could speak he had swung down from the window ledge and they were gone.

He called from below, diminishingly faint. 'I will teach her to dance, Miranda!'

She stood a long time watching the curtains billow

around the broken window. At last, the candle failed and the room was dark again.